FLOOD AND FANG

The Raven Mysteries

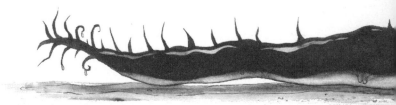

FLOOD AND FANG

The Raven Mysteries

Book 1

MARCUS SEDGWICK

Illustrated by Pete Williamson

Orion
Children's Books

First published in Great Britain in 2009
by Orion Children's Books
a division of the Orion Publishing Group Ltd
Orion House
5 Upper St Martin's Lane
London WC2H 9EA
An Hachette UK Company

1 3 5 7 9 10 8 6 4 2

Text copyright © Marcus Sedgwick 2009
Illustrations copyright © Pete Williamson 2009

The rights of Marcus Sedgwick and Pete Williamson to be identified as
the author and illustrator of this work respectively have been asserted.

The Orion Publishing Group's policy is to use papers that are natural,
renewable and recyclable products and made from wood grown in
sustainable forests. The logging and manufacturing processes are
expected to conform to the environmental
regulations of the country of origin.

A catalogue record for this book is available from the British Library.

ISBN 978 1 84255 692 4

Printed in Great Britain by
CPI Mackays, Chatham ME5 8TD

www.orionbooks.co.uk

For Ravens everywhere

One

Castle Otherhand is
home to all sorts of
oddballs, lunatics
and fruitcakes.
It's just as well
for all of them that
they have a secret
weapon: he's
called Edgar.

I suspect I may have fleas again.

It is altogether a distinct possibility. What do they expect? Keeping me cooped up in this nasty old cage, or maybe allowing me to flap around the High Terrace, with its crumbling, weed-infested stones, it's hardly surprising that I pick up the occasional visitor, is it? It's not my fault. When awake, I spend as much time as I can rootling about with beak and claw, hunting the little chaps down, but I'm an old raven, and my neck hurts if I twist it too far. So then I think to myself, well, one or two visitors will just have to stay till next rootle, and I give up. It's not even as if they taste very nice.

Anyway, as I said, I'm an old raven, and I don't want to get into any more scrapes and scraps, but I suspect I always will.

The Otherhands are all so very stupid, even for people, and it looks very much as though I will have to go on getting this family out of the messes they get themselves in.

Take last Wednesday. Wednesday, never a good day if you think about it, began with the idiot boy, Cudweed, shrieking at the top of his voice that I'd escaped again. I swear he has it in for me at the moment, because of his pet monkey, Fellah. Ridiculous name for a monkey. I know it and you know it. But the truth is that Cudweed was taking misplaced revenge for his *own* naming, which was his parents' fault, of course. Actually, it was his mother alone who named him Cudweed, having previously allowed her husband to name their first born, Cudweed's sister, Solstice. This is only to be expected from a couple called Valevine and Minty. In case you're wondering, Valevine is the head of the household, our lord and master. He really is a lord too, Lord Valevine Plantagenet Vesuvius Ropey Otherhand of Otherhand Castle.

Minty is his wife, the Lady Otherhand. Minty isn't her real name. That would be absurd. Her real name is Euphemia. Minty is one of those awful nicknames which people in love give each other. They're called pet names, but you wouldn't even call a pet monkey Minty.

You shouldn't call it Fellah either, but Cudweed had accurately assessed that nothing would irritate his father more than a name based in slang, and he was right. Slang has the power to irritate Lord Valevine beyond all reasonable measure, as does the dropping of Hs at the start of words, and something he refers to in a low and shaking voice as the 'glottal stop'. I have no idea what one of those is, but it sounds like it might hurt.

The monkey was a tenth birthday present, so no one could object to Cudweed's choice, but 'Fellah' was enough to get Cudweed banished to his room for a week, while Valevine stormed off to his laboratory in the East Tower and didn't emerge for two.

Cudweed is under the impression that I do not like his monkey, but he is wrong.

I hate his monkey.

I hate its continual gabber, and I hate its oggly eyes, and I hate its stupid little red waistcoat. I hate that most of all. But Solstice would tell me off if she knew what I was saying. She'd tell me that hate is a strong word, so let me just say instead that if I had the chance, I'd kill that monkey at the slightest opportunity.

Last Wednesday, therefore, when the bespectacled Cudweed spotted me flapping into the dining hall, he wasted no time in shrieking at the top of his voice.

'He's out again! Mother! Edgar's escaped again!'

Cudweed's not a bad child really. He has thin, short sticky hair, and thick glasses, which make his eyes look very small. He has eaten altogether a few too many of Cook's pies, and while he is not fat, he'd go down a treat on a stranded Antarctic expedition. Most of all, the poor boy is frightened. Always. He is fantastically, extraordinarily, amazingly, award-winningly scared, all the time.

He shivers through life, and right now, he's scared that I might do something to the monkey. Which I would, except I think Fellah might wring my neck if I let him get within arm's grab.

Now, as soon as Cudweed piped up, Fellah joined in and very soon the whole house was ringing to the sounds of stamping feet and shouts of 'There he is!' and 'Shut that window' and 'Where's the net gone?'

Then the cursed castle had to get involved, and suddenly all my routes were shut; not a window or door open to me. I was trapped in the scullery. I swear the castle picks on people sometimes, I really do, but why it was siding with the Otherhands that morning, and not me, I do not know. I've been here much longer than they have, for one thing.

I must have had the whole family and half the kitchen staff staring up at me as I sat on a beam near the ceiling.

They shouted and pointed, and I'm not afraid to admit that I got rather cross, and turned my back on the lot of them. It wasn't as if I had escaped for no reason, but some people just don't want to be helped. There are times when they simply don't seem to realise that I am their guardian angel.

I tucked my beak under my left wing, settled in for a good sulk, had a small rootle, and then it went quiet underneath me, and I heard Solstice call.

'Edgar?' she said. 'Edgar? Won't you come down?'

The devil take me, I don't know what it is about that girl, but suddenly I didn't feel so cross anymore, and I shuffled round on the beam and looked down.

Maybe it's her hair. It's long and shiny and black, as black as the feathers of old Mrs Edgar; black and shiny as coal, right up to the very day she fell off the tree and the dogs ate her. Happy days.

Solstice takes after her mother, or rather, her mother when she was young and interesting. A strange side to the family, Solstice and her mother, and Minty's mother, Grandmother Slivinkov, who lives in an attic high in the castle rafters. She's rarely seen, but that's fine by me, for she is a rather odd old lady,

if I may be polite about it.

'Come down, Edgar,' Solstice said, her voice all lovely like warm milk, and she lifted her arm up towards me. I caved in and jumped down from the beam, landing on her wrist with only a slight stumble. I twitched my beak a bit as if I'd meant to do it, and let Solstice take me back to the cage in the Red Room, behind the High Terrace.

'There, there, Edgar,' she crooned, and listening to her sweet voice, and being quite an old raven, I began to drift off, and completely forgot why I'd been flapping around downstairs in the first place, what I'd seen out in the grounds, and what I'd smelt in the cellars.

Solstice gently popped me back on my perch, and clicked the door shut, locking it with the miniature padlock, and off she went, wondering to herself.

'How do you get out of there, Edgar? It's like magic.'

It's true, they will insist on locking me in the cage, 'so he doesn't hurt himself', and even Solstice, the smartest of them all, is at a loss to explain my excursions elsewhere.

She'd barely shut the door, when suddenly I caught a whiff of that smell again, and it all flooded back into my little bird brain.

'Futhork!' I squawked, which in raven speech is quite rude. I would have to take matters under my wing.

I tilted my head up to the top of the cage and, checking no one was around, flicked the little brass section of bars that secretly opens when pushed just so, and hopped out onto the rug.

Well, that will teach them to buy a second-hand cage from a retired magician, and besides, I have one or two tricks of my own.

Two

The castle was
besieged 32
times before the
Otherhands
'acquired'
it from the
Deffreeques. No one
knows why they
succeeded where the
others failed.

Let me tell you about The Thing I Saw . . .

No! Wait.

The castle.

Perhaps you
need to know a
little about the
castle first.

Castle Otherhand
has been owned and ruled by the Lords of
Otherhand for over three centuries. Before that it
belonged to some family of French origin called
Deffreeque, but the story goes that the third
Lord Otherhand took a liking to the castle and
decided to move his family in. According to the
official *History of Otherhand*, there followed an
altercation, and after that, the Otherhands

moved in. That was all a long time ago, and it's a peaceful place now, by and large, but remnants remain from those troubled days, here and there. The armoury is still sharp and shiny, there are iron pots which once contained hot oil on the battlements and murder holes in various passageways still wink at you as you flap by.

The whole edifice is set on a small plateau on the side of a mountain. It's mountain above, and valley below, and when I sit on the High Terrace, I can see seven counties laid out before me. The castle is a mess, architecturally speaking. I suppose once upon a time there was just one big building sitting up here, but over the years Deffreeques and Otherhands added new wings, extra towers, numerous chapels, halls and so on and so forth, making the current castle a giddy collection of stone and glass. I'm supposed to confine my activities to the Red Room and the High Terrace, a little patch of lawn a full four hundred feet above ground level, but I have Other Favourite Places. I like sitting on the window ledge at the top of the East Tower, right outside the room where Valevine does his experiments, but if I do I have to keep quiet. One squawk and he leans out of the window and bats me away with a

retort stand or an alembic, or whatever else comes to hand. I also like sitting on the little pointy bit on top of the Rotunda, a round room that hugs the south-western corner of the Great Hall, with a domed roof, made in dozens of sections of glass. The sun shines off the panes and the sparkling lights are really pretty, at least to this old raven's eyes.

The castle has about a half acre of bedrooms, almost as many bathrooms, the Great Hall, the Library, the Ballroom, the Kitchens and Scullery. There's the Rotunda, the 'lost' South Wing, the High Terrace, the East Tower, and then there are the bits which people don't like to talk about. I mean, of course, the cellars; vast cavernous vaulted cellars which no one's ever quite got to the bottom of. Then, underneath the cellars, are the caves, and they are ancient and dark places, and even I will not talk about them for very long. It shall suffice to say that the whole castle was built on the side of a mountain riddled with holes. There have been one or two 'incidents' over the years, things involving talons and tentacles, for example. Lord Otherhand keeps promising Minty that he will have every passage and opening into the caves bricked up one of these days, but somehow he never gets round to it, preferring to spend his time on his ludicrous inventions.

But I wish he would do some up-brickery, because there are fey and evil things in those deep caves; it gives me the willies just thinking about it.

And that brings me to the final thing about the castle. No one's ever proved it, not for sure, but the castle has its own habits, if you know what I mean. It has its own views on things; opinions, I suppose. Now that would be fine in itself, but it does tend to get involved sometimes.

Involved.

So that takes me back to last Wednesday, when I was flapping about the dining room like a mentalist, trying to get someone to follow me, so they could see what I had seen.

The trouble was twofold. First, I don't speak human speech. Well not much. I can say a few words, like 'rock' and 'rack' and 'core' and 'hurk' but *you* try having a conversation with that lot. I'm not even sure that 'hurk' is a real word. So if there's something I really need to tell one of them, I usually have to squawk and caw like some stupid crow until they guess what's afoot.

The second problem was that I wasn't sure what I had seen. I'd been flying around, enjoying some late Autumn sunshine, thinking about the chillness of the wind between my feathers. I sat for a while on the ledge on the wall of the East Tower, listening to Valevine explain his latest theory.

As usual, he'd managed to entrap Flinch, the head butler, who was even at that moment holding a bell jar to which were attached two large electrodes. Flinch looked nervous, despite wearing large leather gloves. Inside the bell jar was a frog, who unlike Flinch, was looking rather nonchalant.

'Now then, Flinch,' Valevine said, and he took up a position by my window. I was only just out of sight, so I had to keep very still and absolutely quiet, but in fact I needn't have worried. Valevine was about to begin expounding, and when he expounds, he's in a world of his own dreaming.

'Why is it, Flinch, why is it that we have thunderstorms?'

Flinch didn't reply, but he wasn't

required to. This was an understanding.

'Why do we have thunder? Rain, I understand. Rain is easy. Rain, rain, rain. Easy.'

At this point, Valevine flung the window open so fast I didn't have time to fly away, and found myself pinned against the Tower wall like a specimen under glass. I had fortunately turned

my beak sideways, or it may have been chipped on the glass, and that I wouldn't like to happen, as my beak is, in a word, irreplaceable. I contemplated shuffling along the ledge to escape from my glass prison, when Valevine's head and shoulders emerged through the window. I froze.

His craggy profile jutted out into the thin air high above the valley. Grey hair clung to his scalp like the weeds do the stones of the High Terrace, his black collar swept up so it touched his ears.

'Rain,' he said. 'There is water in the lake, the sun shines, it evaporates, and then when there's too much of it in the sky, it falls back down again. Easy. But thunder? Thunder is not so obvious, my dear Flinch, not so obvious at all.

And yet, I wonder if you have ever noticed a peculiarity of nature concerning the thunderstorm. Think of it.'

Trapped behind the window, and deciding there was nothing else to do for the time being, I thought of it, too.

'The day darkens,' Valevine continued. 'The air thickens, no? You can almost feel it. It hangs heavy like a shroud on an ancient coffin, and the valley is suddenly still. Sounds come from afar; the lowing of the cow, the call of the curlew from the lake, the bark of the bullfrog.'

'The croak, Sir.' I nearly toppled off the ledge, glass prison or not, as Flinch spoke. Most unusual occurrence.

'What?' Valevine turned back from the window, allowing me to stretch an aching wing, 'What did you say?'

'The *croak* of the bullfrog, perhaps, Sir?'

Valevine snorted.

'Yes. But it doesn't alliterate, does it?'

He gave a small snicker of triumph and then his voice took on a whole new sort of mystical, far-away tone.

'The bark of the bullfrog, Flinch. Have you never considered that before every thunderstorm, there comes to the castle walls the majestic bark of the bullfrog? Hah! It is so. The frog barks; his call bounces off the cliffs of the mountain, and is magnified as in an ear trumpet, and thus returns to us as thunder.'

He paused, waiting for an ovation that didn't come. I pictured Flinch solemnly holding the frog in the bell jar with its electrodes.

'And the lightning, Sir?' Flinch ventured.

Valevine snorted again.

'Yes, yes, yes. It is clear that since the sound of the thunderstorm emits from the bullfrog, then so must the lightning itself be produced by our admirable amphibian. But! Flinch, and I am way ahead of you here, why does not the frog emit sparks of light at all times, day in and out? Well, my friend Flinch, that is what we are here to discover. It is my contention . . . '

Here his voice dropped to a portentous whisper.

' . . . that the frog only emits lightning

when the air pressure has rapidly risen and fallen,

as during a thunderstorm.

And, voilá!
Our experiment begins!'

With that Valevine was gone, and I dared to shuffle out from behind the window.

Deciding to leave them to it, I suddenly found myself falling through space. It took me a good long second or two to realise that my wings had gone to sleep and I had set off without getting the blood going again. Contemplating a rapid end on the flags of the Small Courtyard three hundred feet below me, I wondered if this was what had happened to old Mrs Edgar that fateful windy day with the tree and the dogs. Fortunately, not a moment too soon, my trusty wings began to pump away again, and I soared pretty majestically back into the air, my tail feathers merely brushing

the stones of the
courtyard. As
I struggled
back into
the sky, I
saw Solstice
gazing at me
from her bedroom
window, and I flicked my beak about, to make
sure she realised I had meant the whole thing.
It was a flick that said, yes, we old ravens often do
such death-defying feats, and we care little for
such base notions as fear and what-have you.
I'm sure she understood.

She lifted a hand in a wave, and the sun
glinted off a bracelet at her thin wrist, a favourite

piece of her jewellery; silver skulls
with sparkly crystals for eyes.

I flew low over the castle, and wheeled
around for a saunter about the gardens.

Below me I spied Spatchcock, the gardener,
doing his gardening business, piling deadwood
onto a bonfire, and then, from the corner of my
eye, I saw **it.**

A hideous, horrible, hateful thing.

A tail. An absolutely huge tail, glistening
black and **slimy** .

It disappeared, following whatever
owned it, into the undergrowth by the castle
wall, and was gone.

Don't ask me why, but I sensed trouble.

I flew down to the bushes into which the
thing had vanished, and perched on a branch.
A high one, obviously.

I heard nothing, but, bravely and briefly
dropping to the floor of the undergrowth, I was
horrified to see a dark tunnel leading away under
the castle walls, one that I had certainly never
seen before.

I hopped to the mouth of the tunnel, and in short succession three things happened.

First, I smelled a dreadful smell. A smell of rotting decaying meat, and, as one whose main diet *is* rotting meat, let me assure you that this was the most foul odour ever to linger in the nostrils of bird, beast or man. It was carried to me on another aroma, a perfectly normal aroma, one so common that humans don't even seem to smell it. It was the smell of water, and yet somehow, in that dark tunnel, it was unsettling and menacing.

Secondly, there came a rumbling belch of gas being released, something like when a pig which has been dead for four weeks pops, and thirdly, I got very, very frightened, and flapped out of that hole as fast as I could, and began my rampage round the castle looking for help.

And, as it turned out, I was right to do so.

Very, very right.

Three

Lord Valevine
is an inventor
extraordinaire; he
is the inventor of
self-boiling oil, the
square wheel, and
the invisible arrow.
He also claims to
have invented
sneezing.

I have explained what I saw in the bushes by the castle wall, and how that sent me scuttling round the castle trying to get people's attention, and how I freed my feathery self from the far-too-small cage in the Red Room.

But I have not explained what happened later that Wednesday, which really put my tail feathers in a spin.

Upon emerging from my little prison, I noticed the glass doors to the High Terrace were firmly shut, but Solstice had left the door from the Red Room to the passage outside ajar. I hopped over to the gap and listened to the sound of her footsteps retreating. Satisfied that she'd gone, I stuck my beak and then the rest of my head through the crack, and stalked into the castle.

Now don't get me
wrong, ravens can walk,
we can walk perfectly
well. It's just that it looks
a little silly, and for this
reason, we tend to do it
only when there's no one
around to see. I was in
luck. The castle seemed as
dead as I'd ever known it.

I took a few steps over the fading carpet in the
corridor, and twisted my head slightly. This is
a thing ravens do sometimes, and can mean a
variety of things. It can mean 'I'm listening for
something', it can mean 'what you just said was
preposterous', it can mean 'I have a stiff neck',

but in this case it meant 'I have caught a scent and I am trying to ascertain from whence it comes'.

It was that simple smell I'd detected earlier in the day. Water.

I told myself I was being silly. Water does not have an evil smell, and I daresay it's only creatures like dogs and birds who can smell it at all. I would think monkeys are far too brainless to smell anything other than each other's bottoms.

Excuse me, but it's true.

I told myself I was being a foolish old raven. After all, castles are damp places at the best of times, but nevertheless, I couldn't shift the sense of unease what with the watery odour, on top of seeing that terrible tail in the bushes.

My head tilting trick worked a treat,

because I got a powerful whiff which tickled the back of my beak, and set off in pursuit of the smell. I walked to the top of the staircase that led into the gallery running round the Small Hall, and checked again for possible spies. Seeing none, I swooped elegantly across the whole diagonal of the hall, and felt sorry there'd been no one to see it. But had there been, I would have shortly been incarcerated in my cage once more, so it was for the best. I arrived on the ground floor near the corridor to the kitchens, landing on the back of a mouldy padded armchair at only my second attempt.

I spun around. Still nothing.

I was about to turn towards the kitchens, when I detected the source of the  smell coming from underneath me. I hopped to the rug, sniffing, and turned a full circle until I found myself looking at the fireplace, an enormous hearth in which whole cows could, and indeed have, been roasted on a spit, though not recently, you understand. Cook tends to do things more modestly these days, but nonetheless, it was a fireplace with big ideas, though at this particular moment, devoid of fire.

It was from there that the smell was coming.

I stalked over, not forgetting to keep one eye over my shoulder for interlopers, and found myself standing inside the fireplace.

'Well, Edgar,' I said to myself, 'here you are looking at the inside of a fireplace. Perhaps they're right to lock you up after all, eh?'

But as I was chastising myself for being a silly goose of a raven, my eyes spotted something in the darkness of the fireplace. A hole. Quite a large hole, about the height of two Edgars, nestled into the brickwork in the left-hand side of the hearth. I approached the hole, and expecting it to go up, like a chimney, was surprised to find that it plummeted down.

From where I stood, the smell was overwhelming, and I suppose it made my birdbrain swim a little, because the next thing I knew I'd missed my footing, and was falling into total inky black darkness.

'Futhork!' I squawked, for the second time that day, as I tried to flap my way out of trouble. Now I don't know if you've ever tried flying in darkness, but it's actually quite hard. It's very important when you're flying to know which way is up. A moment's thought will tell you it sort of defeats the purpose if you don't, and while you might be tempted to think that the passage of air rushing between your feathers gives you a clue, in the tumbling chaos of my fall into the abyss, I was too confused to think at all.

I batted my wings like a lunatic, but in vain. Seconds later I landed, not on hard ground, but to my way of thinking, on something worse.

Water.

Ravens can fly, and ravens can walk (if there's no one looking), but ravens cannot swim. I have enviously watched my kingfisher cousins dart and play in the river on a summer's day, but this gift is denied to the raven.

I was under for a full few moments of sheer terror. Fighting my way to the surface, I struggled like a bedraggled sailor in the darkness until suddenly I felt something hard under wing, and landed gasping on a sliver of wood poking from the water.

There I lay, shivering the water from my wings, flapping and generally making myself miserable. Gradually, my eyes grew accustomed to the murk and the gloom, and I made an awful discovery.

All around me was water, the source of the smell pervading the castle, and I realised *where* I was, too. In the lower cellars of the castle. The cellars of Otherhand castle are not somewhere I frequent, but I do know that they're not supposed to be flooded. Now I recognised something else. The piece of wood on which I was precariously perching was a door, the top of a door, and only three inches were clear of the water's surface.

I felt my feet go wet.

At this point I think I said, **'Rurk!'** which is not as rude as Futhork, but still a bit, and the reason was this; in the short time I'd been sitting on my three inches of doortop, it had become no inches of doortop. Feverishly, my brain struggled to grasp the significance of my

wet talons, and then . . . **I had it!**
The water was rising.

I could see no way out! The top of my
door had disappeared, and the ceiling of the
lower cellars was coming closer and closer as I
flew frantically round that aquatic dungeon.

I looked for the hole down which I had
tumbled and in my panic I failed and failed to find it.

Then with a squawk of delight I saw a
chink of light coming from a higher doorway at
the far end of the cellar, and darted for it.

The gap between the water and the top of
the doorway was tiny, but I swept through it
majestically, brushing the water with my
wingtips, just like a kingfisher I thought, and
found myself in the upper cellars, safe once more.

Safe, but alarmed.

The castle was in peril. I am its Guardian.

Even as I sat on the steps, I saw the gap through which I had escaped bubble and close, and I knew with a growing dread that I was the only hope for Castle Otherhand.

Four

The fabulous
Lost Jewels of
Otherhand have
been sought by
treasure hunters
for years,
resulting in
frequent unwanted
visitors.

I have mentioned before that I am not as young as the raven I used to be. There were days when I was flea-free, when I could fly from one end of the valley to the other and back to the castle without pausing for breath, when my feathers were all superbly black like wet velvet, and when I never feared evil things.

As I sat in the dim light of the upper cellar, I knew those days were long gone, and my poor bones complained bitterly as I forced them to flap my way out of trouble.

The worst thing you can do when wet is to sit around moping, and with a few flaps of wing, aided by the magical oiliness of raven feather, I was dry again. Furthermore, it is my firm belief that nothing exercises the mind like exercise of body, so as I stood on the step, beating my wings, I felt the start of an idea pop into my head. I wouldn't even have called it a notion at that point, but it was perhaps an egg of sorts, the sort of egg from which notions hatch.

One thing ravens can't do, under any circumstances, is smile. Not because they don't want to; it's a question of beaks, but had I been able to smile, I would have grinned like a monkey swallowing a plate. Sideways.

Delighted, I set off up the steps like a frog in a sock, and flew into the Small Hall once more.

Instantly, my plan was in danger of disaster, for I flew almost entirely into the back of Flinch.

He was walking solemnly along behind Lord Otherhand, who was wagging a finger in the air as he spoke, nineteen to the dozen, but without a backward glance. Flinch didn't seem to be aware that my beak had grazed his butling coat, and plodded on after Valevine.

I l u r k e d.

'More!' Valevine was calling loudly over his shoulder. 'More, and bigger ones! That is the only possible solution to our current failure.'

They were heading towards the front door of the castle.

'I believe the larger ones pass their time

in the western marshes,' Valevine continued,
'And we will bring back a sack load! Heh!'

With that they were through the door
and away. I took up my cause once more, and my
cause led me in one direction only.

The kitchens.

Now I had to proceed with great caution,
because of all the places in the castle I am Not
Supposed To Go, the kitchens are top of the tree.
Furthermore, the kitchens contain the greatest
number of people in the whole of Otherhand.
Not only is this Cook's empire, and not only does

Cook have a myriad of kitchen maids, but being the warmest place in the castle, it's where many of the other servants tend to 'hang out', as they call it. Flinch, if not in his master's shadow, is a frequent visitor here, as are the footmen and any visiting tradesmen.

I knew mine was a difficult path, and yet this was the place I must go, in search of bait.

So far I hadn't even had time to wonder why there was water in the cellars, or where it was coming from, or why it was rising so fast. I knew there were ancient underground rivers in the mountain, for my dear dead mother used to tell me such tales, but why this water had suddenly decided to move upwards into the castle I had no idea.

And then, there was that hideous tail.

I remembered it with a shudder, and I knew this was a dark day indeed.

Girding all the raven courage I could muster, I sailed into the kitchens, gliding magnificently into the rafters of the roasting room.

Someone turned beneath me, and I stood stock still. From the corner of my eye I saw Cook staring up at me, but she didn't really know if she had seen anything or not.

'Cook. **Cook!**'

Minty was screeching at Cook, whose attention I had nearly caught. They were in mid-conversation about something, and Minty is not a woman who likes to be kept waiting.

Minty and Cook. I wanted nothing to do

with either of them. Even if I tried to tell them about the flood, they wouldn't understand. I had a better idea by far.

'Cook! Do pay attention,' Minty pleaded, and with relief I saw Cook turn back to their debate. They were discussing Minty's latest obsession, sponge cakes. On the floor, crawling between the four legs of Cook and Lady Valevine, I saw the twins, dressed as usual in their black romper suits, a last vestige of Minty's former gothic leanings. There was even a little white skull embroidered onto the front of each suit, though frankly their names might have been more use.

One of them, and it might have been Fizz and it might have been Buzz, because to be honest I can't always tell them apart, suddenly stopped its crawling and looked up.

I have no idea why, but the little urchin's eyes were clearly sharper than Cook's, because it immediately pointed and did a fair imitation of my own squawkings.

Cook looked down at Fizz, or Buzz, and a frown appeared on her face.

'Cook,' Minty sighed, 'did you hear me? I don't think you understand how important this is. If I am to make any kind of impression with my sponges, I need variety and I need quantity! Do you understand?'

Cook dragged her fat gaze away from Buzz, or Fizz, and set it back on Minty.

'Do you think it wise to let the little ones loose in the roasting room, your Ladyship?' she said.

Minty sighed again, putting a hand to her forehead as if in great pain.

'No, I suppose not. But they do like to follow me around so. Can't think why, but there it is.'

'Lumber . . . ?' Cook began.

'Nanny Lumber is, I'm afraid to say, taken abed with the flu.'

I wasn't sorry to hear that news. The children's nanny is without doubt the most vicious human I've ever encountered. Even a day in the castle without her presence is a day for sense and justice and hope.

But Cook wasn't to be dissuaded so easily, as even then one of the twins began inspecting glinting carving knives, while the other crawled towards the roasting pit.

'Your Ladyship. Maybe we can talk somewhere less . . . perilous to the small ones?'

'Nonsense, I need to see your cake tins. Are they up to it? Fizz, put that down. Well, what about one of your maids?'

Cook sighed, but nodded, then emitted a fulsome shriek.

'Ishbel! Ishbel come here this minute!'

Nothing happened for a good long while, until a kitchen maid trotted in from the pastry room.

'Who are you?' Cook roared. 'You're not Ishbel, are you?'

The kitchen maid shivered as she answered.

'No, Cook.'

'Who the devil are you? Where's Ishbel?'

'I'm Jenny,' she simpered, and then seemed to lose the courage to go on.

'And where's Ishbel? She's the only one of

you fit enough to mind these two for half an hour.'

'Ishbel isn't here,' Jenny whimpered.

'What?' Cook said, roasting Jenny where she stood. 'What do you mean by that?'

'She's . . . she's missing, Cook.'

'Missing? Missing! Don't be ridiculous. None of my maids are missing!'

'Beg your pardon, but none of us have seen her since Monday teatime.'

That stopped Cook dead. Minty was dragging one of the black-suited ankle-biters away from a pot large enough to boil it whole, and had only half-heard the conversation.

'What? Who's missing?'

Cook seemed suddenly thoughtful.

'Ishbel, your Ladyship. Hasn't been seen since day before yesterday.'

'Who's Ishbel?'

'One of my girls,' Cook said. 'Quite pretty. Not as stupid as some. Gone missing.'

'I see,' Minty said, drawing herself up to her full height of five feet nothing, preparing for action. 'I see. Now, if you'll be so kind as to get this girl here to take the twins off for five minutes, perhaps you can show me your greasing arrangements . . .'

I sat in the rafters, and gave an almighty shudder.

Water rising in the cellars, foreign tails in the caves, kitchen maids going missing, and the family too stupid to know or care.

I saw my chance to act. While Cook scolded Jenny, and Minty chased after Fizz and Buzz, I swooped, pulled a tasty piece of pork crackling from a nearby roasting pig, and vanished from the scene with some style.

Phase one accomplished, the game was on!

Five

Solstice perpetually
wears a ribbon
round her neck,
ever since she
attended her first
'Vampire Ball' and
came home with two
neat puncture marks
in her neck.

Imagine a world without ravens. Pretty frightening stuff, no? And yet that is the awful future I saw before me, as I hunted round the castle with the crackling in my beak. For what would happen if I were to fail in my mission, and Otherhand were swept away by floodwaters, and the survivors polished off by the creature with the tail? A creature with a tail of that nature clearly has vicious teeth at its other end, and all sorts of terrifying images galloped into my bird brain.

I pictured a great variety of nasty outcomes, and as I said, it was pretty frightening stuff, these images. Images of flood and fang.

Ha! Yes, it's all getting scary, I thought, but this isn't the first time I've been called to save the castle, and it won't be the last. Telling myself I'd seen worse (perhaps), I stuck my beak in the air and cawed, to give me courage.

It was time to put phase two of my plan into action.

Now, normally, there's no getting away from that odious primate, that chattering hairball, that filthy monkey, Fellah. Usually he dogs my every waking minute at Otherhand; leering at me, trying to grab my tail feathers, throwing things at me as I soar above him and generally giving me no peace. So it was even more typically irritating of him that the one time I was actually looking for him, he was nowhere to be found.

I flew from the top of the castle to the bottom, to the top again, and perched on the pointy bit of the rotunda while I thought where to fly next. Then I flew from the East to the West and round by the South, and still nothing.

On my expedition I sighted many of the other inhabitants of Otherhand, but I would be blasted if I could find that monkey anywhere. I saw Spatchcock, still out in the gardens as usual. As I wheeled overhead he was ferreting about under the gigantic leaves of the rhubarb patch. He seemed intent on extracting something that lay in their sweet shade. But Fellah was not present, so I couldn't waste time with Spatchcock's fumblings.

I slid on through the sky and saw Solstice sitting on the High Terrace, scratching with pen and ink in her notebook. More sombre poetry, was my guess, and I wished a smile on her lips and a song in her heart, but there was no time for me to stop and settle on her shoulder, as I know she likes, because I still had to find Fellah.

She looked up, saw I had escaped, and seemed about to shout at me when she changed her mind. She smiled and waved.

With Solstice's blessing, I felt a surge of energy, and pushed through the air with startling

vigour for a bird of my advanced years, and yet,
I still had to find that monkey.

In my desperation I even sought him in
the East Tower. I landed on the windowsill and
peered cautiously in, putting the crackling down
carefully on the ledge as I did so, for my beak
had grown stiff holding it, and if I'm honest, the
temptation was growing to gobble it up, fly off to
some nice new castle and leave the Otherhands
to their own miserable doom.

I suppose I was a bit overtired by now
and when I get tired I admit that I can become a
little difficult, a little grouchy. I stared gloomily
through the window, my attention taken by
Valevine and Flinch and their wild experimentations.

They'd returned from the marshes and

seemed to have been successful
in their hunt for larger ones.
Bullfrogs, that is.

One sat stony-faced in a glass bell
jar a few feet from my perch. He seemed
disinterested in the goings-on around him,
whereas Valevine was all astir and even Flinch
was concentrating on winding a large wooden
handle, that was attached to an equally large
contraption standing on the floor. Bellows rose
and fell, and from this apparatus, two long flexible
hoses, about the width of a sheep's head, snaked
over to another piece of equipment, a wooden
box on the table beside the frog. From here,
Valevine attached two small versions of the
snaking tube to the bell jar, as well as some copper

wires which clipped neatly onto the electrodes
I'd witnessed earlier that day.

'Pump, man, pump!' Valevine exhorted
Flinch. 'I want you to wind like you have never
wound before!'

Flinch moved faster than I had ever seen,
and the bellows bellowed and the tubes twitched
in readiness.

I was just checking on my pork crackling,
wondering whether or not it was sensible to
abandon my ancestral home of
hundreds of years for the
sake of a snack,
when Valevine
flicked a switch
on the box.

There was a loud and rather final noise
from inside the laboratory, a sort of sucking pop,
so sudden that I nearly fell off that window ledge
for a second time. I whirled back to see what
had happened.

Poor frog. He appeared to have vanished,
and in his place inside the bell jar was a rather
messy pool of red goo, much of which was pasted

on the inside of
the glass.
Valevine was
staring hard at
the contents.
He turned to
Flinch, sighing
gravely.

'What
more can we do?
The pressure has
become unimaginable, and still not a single peep
of thunder, never mind a spark of lightning!
What more can we do, Flinch?'

Flinch didn't answer but merely began
wiping, while Valevine turned to the box of frogs

sitting on the laboratory floor.

'Who's next?' he asked brightly.

That was more or less when I knew for sure that a small sparrow has more brains than the entire Otherhand clan put together, and more chance of saving them from doom than they have themselves.

Like the frog, it made me feel a little gooey myself, to think that they needed me so much, even if they didn't know it.

Steely determination in my heart and pork crackling in my beak, I dropped like a stone, picking up a fearsome speed which I then translated into an impressive horizontal velocity, and within seconds, I found my quarry.

It was still an hour to lunchtime, but I remembered it was Cudweed's habit to arrive in the dining hall in plenty of time before lunch, to make sure he didn't miss out on anything in the way of food. Sure enough, I found the boy and the dratted monkey fooling about with cutlery. The time had come.

I landed square on the long dining table, sending a couple of glasses crashing to the floor as I did. Flying, and landing, are not always as easy as I make them look.

There, only feet away, and far too close for comfort, sat Fellah, in his irritating tiny red waistcoat, swatting at the air like a lunatic swats at imaginary flies. My arrival stopped him in

his tracks, and he turned his yellow saucer eyes towards me.

It was a stand-off for a few seconds. I stared at the monkey, the monkey stared at me, and Cudweed looked from one of us to the other and back again, his poor brain realising something was afoot, but not yet realising what that foot was.

I waggled the crackling in my beak, and now the dim primate, Fellah, I mean, understood: I had food. I was waving it at him.

And if he lunged fast enough he just might get it.

He lunged, I ducked, and scrabbled with clacking claws to the table's edge.

Now the room was all noise and commotion as Fellah let out a long howl and began to chatter like a roomful of kitchen maids. He hissed and swore, pointed and swatted, and came for me again.

I was playing a dangerous game, letting him come close enough to think he might get the pork, without actually letting that happen. He lunged again, and Cudweed yelped with panic as his monkey sent three more crystal glasses shattering on the stone floor. If his mother, or worse, Cook, or worst of all, Nanny Lumber found out, there would be hell to pay.

But I took no heed, for greater things were in the air, and I knew I must enrage and entice the monkey so much that he would lose all reason.

It didn't take long, and by the time I had let him lunge, and miss, for a third time, I judged he was about ready, so when I flapped slowly out of the dining room, just above monkey-jumping height, Fellah scrambled after me, gibbering like, well, like a monkey.

My plan was working!

Six

The most fabulous
item of the Lost
Jewels is 'the Luck of
Otherhand', a huge
solitaire diamond
that weighs as much
as a fully grown
raven. And he
should know.

So far, so good, but this was merely the start of the chase, for what I had in mind would need more than a stunted baboon chasing me. As I swooped round the doorpost, I risked a backwards glance, and saw with unnatural delight that Cudweed was also scampering after me. But Cudweed is an unreliable boy. I needed more.

Trying to solve the problem, my poor old raven brain struggled like a crocodile's lunch, but moments later I had the solution. Back to the kitchens! Nowhere else in the castle might I find so many people, and be able to cause so much chaos.

Dropping one wingtip I executed a splendid quarter circle

and now my heading was South and the smell of the kitchens wafted towards me once more.

Lunch was about to be served and the place was in utter chaos, what with Cook and countless maids and various flunkeys.

I am a shadow, I have to admit it. There's no point being modest on this one; I am a black, unseen shadow when I want to be, and though I can squawk with the best of them, you try squawking with your beak full of crackling. Thus it was that my entry to the forbidden realm went unseen and unheard, but fortunately I didn't have long to

wait before the boy
and the monkey
burst into the
room, and I'm
not the only one
who fears that hairy
little beast. I mean Fellah,
not Cudweed, because at
that second, a shrill wail went up from
the first kitchen maid to hand, who dropped a
steaming soup tureen. The noise and mess was
utterly tremendous, more than I could have
hoped for really, and within another half second
the whole room was alive with shouts, screams,
crashes and bangs.

'Get that blasted monkey out of here!'

That was Cook, and even above the din, her voice put the fear of the Devil into everyone. A dozen pairs of feet scrambled after the monkey, but Fellah was too quick for them, and I was too quick for him. I dipped under the doorway and was thrilled to see Solstice and her mother descending the stairs, wondering where their lunch had got to. Solstice saw me streak back into the hall, all feathers flying, followed by a leaping monkey, a sweating boy, and a gaggle of kitchen maids. She tossed her head and laughed out loud, her long black hair flicking dust from the candelabra as she did.

Minty was less pleased, though, I think,

for she shrieked like I've never heard anyone shriek before. She spat words out like bullets, each one a terrible murderous blow.

'Catch! That! Monkey!'

I was even more pleased with this, because for once the monkey was in trouble, not me. I tried to smile, but as I may have mentioned, ravens cannot smile, and all that happened was that I dropped the crackling, the bait, from my foolish beak.

I tried to swoop for it before a dozen hands grabbed me, but I need not have worried. Fellah's brain, which after all is only the size of a small walnut, was now so enraged that he had forgotten why he was chasing me, and only wanted one thing, to put his rubbery hands around my glossy black neck.

I made a turn about the hall, for I'd missed the doors to the cellars on my first pass, and the whole chain of diving, crashing people hurtled after me. People are not as good as birds at turning corners, I ruminated, as with each turn I made, another priceless vase or valuable piece of armour went clattering and smashing to the stone floor.

'Solstice!' screamed Minty, **'Do something!'**

And so there was Solstice chasing me too, and a couple of footmen and even Flinch himself were on my tail. Lord Valevine appeared at the head of the stairs, coming to see what all the row was about. I noticed grimly that he still wore some large white protective gloves, and wondered how many more poor frogs had evaporated in his infernal machine that morning.

I turned for the cellar steps. As I followed my speeding beak into the darkness, a dread-inducing scream echoed down the steps behind me.

Never mind! I thought. Pay no heed! Your work is nearly done. And then I was there, at the edge of the terrible water, which I noticed was now even higher than when I'd left it. Now the dim humans would see their fate, and admire and recognise the noble efforts of one poor heroic raven. I flung myself high out of reach on a beam, and turned.

My beak nearly fell off in shock.

Only the boy and the monkey had followed me down the steps, with Cudweed barely managing to overcome his fear because of his unbalanced concern for Fellah.

Every single last one of the others had stayed in the hall.

I could have cried. My wings ached as if they might drop off, and below the monkey jabbered and pointed as it tried in vain to climb up to my beam.

It managed to get a couple of toe holds on the cellar walls, then slipped back down again, too angry to do anything sensible. Cudweed hopped about and tried to catch Fellah, but this was more exercise than he'd had all year, and he wasn't quite up to the challenge.

Neither of them even noticed the water lapping where the cellar should have been, and neither seemed likely to either.

That's it! I thought. That really is it, this time! Let them all drown!

And with that, I turned my back on boy and monkey, tucked my beak under my wing, and wondered how long to sulk for.

Seven

It's said there are 52 staircases in Castle Otherhand, one for every week of the year, and 366 rooms, one for every day in a leap year, but no one's ever managed to count them all properly.

Consider the fish.

The fish in the river.

There they are, doing fish-based things,
going about their fishy business, swimming and
whatnot, eating smaller fish, I suppose, occasionally
winking at sexy lady fish, and generally being
wet. And all the while, they are completely
unaware of the world above the water, until one
day, a kingfisher darts into their realm and snatches
them away, and just at the very moment they
realise there is a whole other world beyond
theirs, they're dead, swallowed whole by a
greedy bird.

You see my point?

Yes, that's just how I felt about the family.
I had done my very best to warn them, but not

only were they totally ignorant of their imminent demise, they seemed utterly ignorant too of my own existence. I was to them as the tree on the riverbank is to the fish.

My thoughts ran dark and deep as I warmed my beak under my wing on that high beam.

As I sat there, I heard, or maybe rather felt, a low, deep rumbling coming from the bowels of the castle. More badness, I thought, but it passed soon enough, and besides, I was busy sulking.

I will stay here until I die, I thought,

possibly longer, and then they'll be sorry. Then they'll miss old Edgar. So I settled in to spend the rest of my days on that miserable perch, but after about five minutes my neck really began to ache, and I decided not to die there after all.

I flapped off the beam in such a way as to express deep contempt for Cudweed and his monkey, and I felt pretty sure I had secured a victory of sorts, though just don't ask me to explain exactly how. But boy and pet had grown tired and sloped off somewhere. Unimpeded, I flew lazily back up to the Small Hall.

Expecting the crowd to have dispersed, I now received a second shock in a sadly short time. There they all stood, in a great circle, around something, or someone, on the threadbare polar bearskin rug in the centre of the hall.

I swooped to perch on the dust-encrusted bust of the first Lord Deffreeque, who built the castle, in order to gain a better view.

The entire population of the castle stood in that hall, I swear.

Lord and Lady Otherhand, Solstice, the twins, Cook, Flinch, every other butler, maid, footman and flunkey I've ever laid my sooty eyes on. But most surprising of all, and as I saw him, my beak dropped open, was

Spatchcock, the gardener. In all his days at Otherhand I had never once seem him inside the castle. He stood, dressed as ever in his grey and green gardening apparel, down to his muddy black Wellingtons.

On the bearskin lay the prostrate form of a kitchen maid, but no one was the slightest bit interested in her. Jenny, I think it was, and she was still breathing, so she must have fainted. Either that or she was very tired, but then I remembered the scream I'd heard as I'd tried to take everyone downstairs, and a picture of what was happening began to form.

Everyone's eyes were on Spatchcock.

This in itself was unusual, for Spatchcock is a quiet and solitary old goat, who keeps himself to himself, who works the ornamental and kitchen gardens all day every day, and who sleeps in his potting shed down at the end of the garden wall. Though a familiar sight around the grounds, he is a distant one, and Valevine was not alone in struggling to remember the venerable gardener's name.

Yet, here he was, the centre of attention. And all because, in his hands, he held a pair of boots.

Now, you have probably realised what a remarkably astute bird I am, so it won't surprise you to learn that I could immediately deduce a few things from the scene below.

The boots were not Spatchcock's. For a start, I could see his own muddy rubber boots on his feet. Secondly, the boots he held aloft were very small, and made of leather. They were without doubt the sort of boots a girl would wear, but not a fine and rich young lady. No, these were small, black, stout working boots, the very sort a maid might wear to go about her daily castle business. Another glance told me that Jenny still wore her boots as she lay in a faint on the polar bear, and you can see that I was rapidly narrowing in on the possible owner of the footwear.

There, however, I admit I was stumped. Until one name floated to me from the hubbub beneath.

'Ishbel! Poor Ishbel!'

Ah ha!

The maid who had gone missing on Monday, and now here were her boots. A terrible crawling sensation began to wriggle through my feathers, perhaps it was fear, perhaps fleas, but I had no time to ponder, for evil lurked in our very midst, it seemed.

My mind raced to the sight of that hideous black slimy tail slithering through the undergrowth, and my fears were confirmed as I snatched at the discussion below me.

'Yes, Ma'am,' Spatchcock mumbled. 'In the rhubarb patch. Yes, both of them. Under a large leaf.'

'You're quite sure?'

'Yes, Ma'am.'

'And no sign of the girl?'

'No sign of nothing else, Ma'am, save for these awful large tracks that led through the rhubarb.'

'Tracks, you say, Satchelpants?'

This was Lord Otherhand himself speaking, names of staff not his strong point.

'Tracks, Sir. Horrible they were, footprints like a wolf, but with only three toes, and a long scrape in the mud between the left and right feet.'

'I see,' said Valevine, 'And where did these tracks go, Sludgepig?'

'Go, Sir?'

'Yes! Where did they go, man?'

'I don't know that I know, Sir. I just picked up the boots and came to find Her Ladyship. Thought you ought to know that something had eaten the girl.'

At this, another maid fainted and two more began wailing and crying.

I sat on Lord Deffreeque's wooden chair, and my poor little raven's heart trembled.

Ishbel, the maid, quite pretty and not as stupid as some, had fallen foul of the beast from below.

The commotion beneath me was simply terrible, and it was with an enormous roar that Valevine finally managed to restore some order to the room.

'Quiet! Silence! That is a command from your Lord and Master!'

At length the only voice was that of Lord Otherhand, and he spoke calmly and with great authority.

'We do not know,' he said, catching every eye in the room, 'that the girl has been eaten. Quiet! Steady there. We do not know this. All we know is that she has been missing for some two days, and that her boots have been recovered from the clutches of that foul fruit, the rhubarb . . .'

'Vegetable, Sir.'

'What?' roared Valevine, turning on Spatchcock.

'Vegetable, Sir, the rhubarb is a vegetable.'

Lord Otherhand seemed thrown for a moment.

'Nonsense,' Minty said.

Valevine, seeing he was losing his audience, hurried on, ' . . . that vile *vegetable*, the rhubarb, and tracks of an unknown creature are to be seen in the vicinity. This does not mean,' he roared again, 'that the girl has been eaten. That would be all too easy an assumption to make. And I will not make an easy assumption while there is breath in my body!'

He paused, expecting an ovation for his rousing speech, but didn't get one.

'Yes, dear,' said Minty, 'but what are we going to do?'

'Look for her!'

This was Solstice, and my heart skipped. At last, there was a chance of sense.

'We must look for her,' she cried again,

and I squawked from on high to show I approved.

'See! Even Edgar agrees! We must organise search parties, and search the castle from top to bottom!'

There was now a loud cheer, and general agreement, and then a small treacly voice piped up.

'Well,' Cudweed said, and I noticed he had wet feet. Fellah clung around his neck, shivering, with a dripping tail. 'Well, there's no point looking at the bottom of the castle.'

'And why not, my boy?' enquired Valevine.

'Because the bottom of the castle is full of water.'

'Nonsense,' said Minty, and then everyone turned at the sound of water running into the hallway from the mouth of the cellar.

Eight

Minty's culinary
passions are a recent
thing; in days of old
she was a witch of
high calibre, known
for her particularly
vicious curses; like
purple wart disease.
No one is very keen
to try her cooking.

Panic is a word often overused, but it would not be a bad word to describe what happened next. At the sight of the water, there was a general commotion, a raucous pandemonium, and a dreadful hullabaloo all at once.

I sat watching everyone, wondering whether it had crossed their minds it was my efforts that had led to the discovery of the water, and then I realised, with disappointment, it hadn't been me who'd shown them the water, after all, but the water that had shown itself, by gurgling up from the cellar steps.

It was extraordinary how fast the water moved, as it flowed across the flags of the hall floor, soaking the polar bear in moments. As it spread across the vast space, it slowed its

pace slightly, but nevertheless people began
running in every direction, shouting all sorts of
idiotic commands.

'Edgar! Edgar!'

Through the din I heard my name being
called gently, and saw Solstice waving up at me.

'Come down here, Edgar.'

I decided not to. I was sulking, after all.

That was my general argument
at that point. I watched with dismay
as the splashing and shouting grew
to a crescendo.

'Open the door!'
screamed Minty.

'No, close it!' shouted Valevine.

'The front door?'

'No, the cellar door!'

'What?'

'I said . . . '

'Has someone left a bath running?'

'Fetch some buckets! And a mop!'

'Get that polar bear off the floor!'

So it went on.

I surveyed the scene again, when suddenly, to my horror, I could feel breathing on the back of my neck. A fraction later I smelled monkey, and it was nothing more than deep inbuilt instinct that made me launch into the clear air of the hallway, where, circling the massive and ancient chandelier that hung there, I saw Fellah screeching at me from the bust of Lord Deffreeque. He'd been about to grab me, and only his rancid monkey aroma had saved me from strangulation!

'Edgar! Edgar!'

Solstice was still urging me to join her, and upon reflection I decided that her companionship might offer me some protection. I swooped and landed on the wrist she held out for me, then hopped along her arm to her shoulder. Before I knew what was happening, Solstice turned and planted a kiss on the tip of my beak, and I blushed from head to talon, a fact which only went unseen because I am covered with feathers. Useful, at times.

I wondered what had got into the girl,

but she was already heading for the door.

'Edgar,' she whispered, her eyes wide with excitement. 'It's up to us now. Do you see? Everyone has forgotten about poor Ishbel already. Even her friends, more worried about getting their boots wet, they are. But she has gone missing, and it's up to us to solve the mystery of her disappearance!'

I fluttered my wings to show I agreed.

'Edgar,' she went on. 'Do you think . . . do you think . . . she has gone, for ever? Do you think she has been eaten? I know Father doesn't agree, but it doesn't look good, does it Edgar? Do you think she's been swallowed whole by something lurking in the rhubarb?'

I did think that. I thought that very much, and so it was with a heavy raven heart that I uttered a mournful syllable.

'**Urk!**'

'Then, Edgar,' Solstice said, as we left the castle doorway, and headed out into the afternoon, 'it is up to us to solve the mystery of the munched kitchen maid, for what has happened once, could happen again!'

And then I did shiver, for until that very second, that particular idea had not entered my feathery braincase. But what Solstice said was true. What if, oh horror, what if the terrible beastie struck again?

And again?

Nine

Solstice's poetry, famed throughout the castle for its gloomy nature, is in fact a remarkably powerful antidote to insomnia. Her favourite piece of her own work is entitled; Why aren't I dead?

'Now!' said Solstice, 'for the rhubarb patch! Come on, Edgar.'

New strength flooded into my wings, and I took flight, scrambling off Solstice's shoulder and leading the way around the side of the castle towards the gardens.

I flapped slowly through the formal gardens, hoping that Solstice, who ran behind me, could keep up. I cruised over the tops of purple and blue lupins, ducked under a rose arbour, and skirted a wide bed of lavender and rosemary.

Frankly I dawdled, and though her straight hair
flew behind her, and she pulled up the skirt of
her long pencil dress so her legs could move
more easily, still Solstice fell behind.

'Edgar!' she called, 'Don't fly off! Wait
for me!'

Something slithering. That's all I had
seen, something slithering, but as we approached
the site of the slither, I wondered what I had
seen, exactly. A tail, and nothing more. And yes,
it had been unnaturally large, and evil-looking,
but almost anything could have been at the front
end of that tail. Was this wise? What had I got
myself involved in?

I stopped, waiting for Solstice to reach
me, perching on a sign that Valevine had instructed

Flinch to put up after the last trespassers had
been caught hunting for that stuff they call the
Lost Treasure of Otherhand.

 said the sign,

It had been Valevine's attempt at humour,
but now it was all too possible.

Solstice finally caught up.

 '**Rurk!**' I said, expressing my doubts
at our plan.

'Yes, Edgar,' she said, standing nose to
beak, 'It is exciting, isn't it? Come on then!

Let's find these tracks.'

Ah well, I thought, I tried.

Solstice was leading the way towards the vegetables, and I could do nothing but follow.

The girl is bright, and certainly knew cabbage from rhubarb. By the time I caught her up she was holding a floppy rhubarb leaf aloft and peering into its shady gloom.

'Gasp!' she said, which was very odd to my way of thinking. Gasping is something humans are supposed to *do*, not *say*. But Solstice has her own way with many things. Poetry, for example.

'**Urk?**' I enquired.

'Yes, gasp, Edgar. Look!'

There in the undergrowth were the tracks that Spatchcock had spoken of.

Footprints, each one the size of Solstice's long pale hands, but with only three toes, and as if that weren't creepy enough, there was the long groove running up the middle, between the left and right sets of tracks. Something glistened here and there in this groove, and Solstice bent down for a closer look.

'Gasp, a third time!' she declared, and plucked something from the mud. It was a scale, shining in the afternoon sunlight, like a small jewel, green and glittery.

So, whatever had made these disturbing tracks hadn't been a three-toed wolf with a strangely large tail, but a scaled beast, like a snake.

But with legs! Perhaps it was one of the dreaded
Glottal Stops that Valevine sometimes talked about.

Whatever it was, I shuddered, and started
to flick my beak this way and that, wary the monster
might return without warning. But Solstice was
not to be deterred, and was already following
the tracks.

She was rapidly heading for the castle
wall, for that very hole from which I had first
detected evil odours and noxious aromas.

I called after her, urging her to be cautious.
'Rark!'

'Yes, come on,' she said, and was at the
mouth of the cave, peering into the darkness,
when I spotted something else in the mud, not a
footprint, nor a scale, but something that really

made my feathers stand on end.

I dropped to the ground and plucked it from the mud with my beak, then hopped over to Solstice, who looked to see what I was fussing about.

This time, even Solstice was too genuinely alarmed to say anything, as she bent over and took the thing from my mouth, a large, vicious, curved fang. A terrifying tooth, as long as one of Solstice's fingers, it was not pure white, but had a rather unpleasant yellowish stain, and had clearly been broken off at its base by some struggle with . . . with what? With poor Ishbel?

'Edgar,' Solstice said slowly, 'I have the most awful idea that whatever owned this fang, probably still owns a lot more of them, if you know what I mean.'

Yes, I did.

'**Rark!**'

First flood, and now fang! What stinking villainy was threatening Castle Otherhand?

'Rark!' I said. 'Rark, rark, rurk, futhork!'

'Yes,' said Solstice. 'Gasp.'

Ten

112,562 arrows were fired during the 32 sieges of Castle Otherhand. Old arrowheads are just some of the strange things frequently found in the castle grounds.

'We must get back to the castle,' Solstice declared. I flapped in agreement.

'But first, we must explore this cave!'

I flapped in disagreement.

Was she unhinged? And besides, it was too dark inside to see anything useful. You  wouldn't even see what ate you.

'Ah ha!' cried Solstice. 'Look!'

Awkward child. The sun was dipping into the afternoon, and as Solstice and I waited, it sank low enough for a beam of light to penetrate the cave mouth.

'Come on, Edgar. I won't be scared with you beside me.'

How considerate of you, I thought to myself.
My good mood had worn off, and I was feeling
very sorry for myself, very sorry indeed. I did not
want to follow poor Ishbel into the maw of the
monster with dripping fangs, and entering that
cave seemed a very good way of doing just that.

But things worked in my favour, for
Solstice had only taken a step
into the cave when she stopped.

'Oh!' she said, 'It's blocked.
There's no way in. But look! This is
where the tracks go.'

It was very odd indeed. Ahead of us was
a solid wall of rocks and boulders, and yet the
tracks were plain enough even in the gloom,
disappearing under the rocks.

Water trickled from underneath the pile, here
and there.

'This must have only recently happened,'
Solstice said thoughtfully, scratching her ear.

I could see she was working things out in her head, and as she did, I suddenly remembered the rumbling noise I'd heard when lurking on the cellar steps with Cudweed and the chimpanzee.

'So!' Solstice said, patting the rocky wall of the cave. 'The castle is fighting back, perhaps? Is that the end of the beast, maybe?'

Squashed by a thousand tons of stone! If this were true, it was no more than it deserved.

I hoped it was true, but then we both remembered that there remained an equal peril to the castle's well being.

The flood!

'Come on, Edgar. Let's get back. We can show them what we found!'

Clutching the fang, we fumbled and

fought our way back out of the darkening cave

and returned in haste to Otherhand Castle.

Eleven

The 'lost' South
Wing of the Castle
is now in great
disrepair, and no
one ever visits;
strange lights are
seen and noises
heard at night.

There are a few things Ravens do not like. Obviously, these things vary from bird to bird, but top of my list would be monkeys. I might follow this with a host of contenders for second place. Small boys, vicious Nannies, baths, fleas and so on, though I'm not even sure about fleas. I mean, were someone to wave a magic wand, and remove them from my life altogether, it makes me wonder what I would do with myself of an evening, with nothing to rootle for. Strange one, that. Bit of a conundrum.

Anyway, you can see that I could spend a long time running through the list of Things I Do Not Like, but as the sun started to set over the castle at dusk last Wednesday, I knew that I would have to be adding another item to my list of dislikes. Namely: unseen, scaly, fang-toting, slithering monsters which ate kitchen maids.

You will notice that I say maids, in the plural, for as Solstice and I came back inside, we were greeted by a renewed wailing and sharp old bird that I am, I knew some new disaster had been unearthed.

'Ann!' someone screamed. 'Where is that girl?'

'Ann!'

'Ann?'

'Ann. Very tall. Blonde, mostly.'

'Oh, *that* Ann. Ann!'

And then someone ran in holding Ann's boots, without Ann inside them, and all manner of rambunctious behaviour ensued.

All this occurred in about a foot of water, which only added to the confusion.

Solstice splashed off, waving the fang at anyone who would listen, and I realised that any hope the creature had perished in the rock fall was probably misplaced. It seemed the beast was still on the prowl, a beast with a hunger for kitchen maids, though not for their boots.

The water in the hall had now reached the front door, and there was a constant stream flowing through it. Those who owned long boots were wearing them, but mostly people were getting rather wet.

Solstice had found her mother, and was asking for her opinion on the fearsome fang we'd found, but Minty was distracted. 'Supposing my sponges become damp?' she kept repeating.

Solstice sent her mother a withering sigh, but spotted Flinch stalking up the stairs, and ran after him, instead.

'Flinch! Flinch!' she called, 'Where's my father? He must see this!'

Flinch paused only briefly.

'Lord Valevine is continuing with his
experiments concerning Thunder, my lady.
He has given strict instructions that he is not to
be disturbed.'

'What?' Solstice exclaimed, 'But the castle
is flooding! Flooding! We are all in mortal danger!'

'Rubbish!' Minty declared. 'Rubbish.
Look, the water is flowing out of the front door.
There is no danger. Well, not to most of the castle.'

'Most of the castle?' Solstice cried. '*Most*
of it?'

'Have you seen my monkey?'

That was Cudweed, without monkey,
I was pleased, if puzzled, to see.

'Have you seen my monkey?

If we're all going to drown I want my monkey.'

'No one is going to drown,' Minty said, 'though I fear for my cake tins.'

'Solstice, have you seen Fellah anywhere?'

'No! I haven't and I don't care!' Solstice wailed.

She sounded slightly hysterical now, I think, because she was tired, her feet were wet, and no one seemed very interested in the fang. I settled on her shoulder, and she jumped.

'Oh! Edgar, it's only you. You scared me, you bad bird.'

But she said it in a kind way and I knew she wasn't really that cross.

'Sometimes, Edgar,' she went on, 'I despair of this family. I really do.'

Cudweed stomped off.

Solstice sighed.

'Do you ever get the feeling that no one is listening to you?'

'**Caw,**' I uttered, mournfully.

'Yes, I know. Me too. Come on, Edgar. I'll put you to bed with some nice dried mice for supper. Would you like to sleep in my room tonight? I could bring your cage in there and we can keep each other company. Yes?'

'**Caw,**' I said again. Too tired to say more, I let Solstice carry me upstairs, and as the sounds of chaos faded away, I tucked my beak into the folds of her black silk sleeve, and was asleep before she even put me in my cage, despite the promise of dried mice.

Twelve

At the Great
Hallowe'en Ball,
Otherhand castle
plays host to all the
noble families of
seven counties. It's
quite a bash, and
there's usually a bit
less silverware when
everyone's finally
gone home.

I woke in the middle of the night, in the unfamiliar surroundings of Solstice's room. It's a small room as Otherhand bedrooms go, but all the cosier for it. There's a wonderful view over the valley from a small octagonal window, and I think that was why Solstice had begged to move here when she grew out of the nursery, having seen the way the full moon shines straight onto the wall opposite the window.

Her room's always full of stuff, lots of books, both to read and to write or draw in, paints, flowers, bits of bark, stones. And darker things; odd plants like mandrake and nightshade, a reel of something that looked like cotton but which I knew was

actually cobwebs, and
bottles of odd coloured
potions that are
unknown to me.
A hotch-potch and
a melting pot of
almost anything. It's the room
only Solstice could have.

But I am rambling away from my story!

I woke. I had been dreaming, dreaming
about the days when poor Mrs Edgar and I were
young and happy. We'd cruise the valleys, exploring
far and wide. These days I'm too tired to get much
farther than the top of our own valley, but I was
quite the bird in those days. Quite the bird. I could
do any number of impressive tricks while flying.

I suppose I was showing off really, but Mrs Edgar used to love it. I could loop the loop and tumble, perform rolls in the air, and then there was my most special trick, a thing which any human would tell you is impossible; flying backwards.

That took some wing power, I can tell you, and Mrs Edgar would slap her wingtips together when I did it, which showed how happy she was.

Rambling again! But the point is, that when I woke in the darkness, my bird brain was miles, and years, away.

I tilted my head.

Everything was quiet. No! Not quite everything.

My ears may be old, but they're still keen

enough to hear a beetle scrabble in the skirting board three rooms away. First, there was the sound of Solstice, softly snuffling in her sleep. I hoped she was having dreams as nice as mine had been. The remains of her supper lay on a tray beside her bed, and one hand trailed in a bowl of sultanas. She'd already spilled the dregs of a glass of milk, but I could do nothing about that, for there were other sounds coming to me, as I tuned into the heartbeat of the night.

The wind, a gentle wind, soughed outside the window. And then I heard something altogether more unsettling. A **padding** and a **slithering**, all at once, and it was coming from the corridor outside Solstice's door. It was far away, but it was coming closer.

At first I wondered if it was more burglars, hunting the Lost Treasure of Otherhand. That sort of thing is not uncommon, but as I listened, I began to sense something more sinister sliding along the passageway.

I froze, trying to be still, praying that Solstice would snore more quietly, and as I did so, I heard a horrible gurgling, breathing, a vigorous snorting and belching combined, and I knew that the beast was patrolling the very corridors of the castle.

I flicked my gaze to the door.

Had Solstice locked it before retiring? I knew she usually did, in the way that girls of a certain age do, but maybe she'd forgotten? I'd been a-slumber already. Could the beast force the door, did it know we were here? Could it smell us, as I could now smell it?

I knew it could, for at that very second, there was a muffled thump against the woodwork, a wet, yet solid thump, insistent and ominous.

It came again and I began to squawk in my cage, rattling the bars with my beak, flicking

seeds and allsorts of muck onto the floor.

I had lost my nerve. Let the thing hear! I thought wildly. Let it come in here and try and

eat me through the bars of my little prison. Hah!
I'd like to see it digest me inside this brassy thing!

Then I remembered Solstice, and saw
that I had woken her.

She stumbled blearily over to me, and I
squawked some more, as if I were some kind of
appalling parrot.

'What is it, Edgar? Are you all right?'

'Rurk!' I said, desperate now to warn her
not to open her door.

'What is it?' she said. 'Are you trying to
tell me something? You clever bird. Did you
hear something? Probably just a bad dream,
but I'll have a look around, to show you, okay?'

'Futhork!'

Poor Solstice went over to the door, dressed in her lovely black nightgown, all floaty and light. Great to sleep in, but bad for stopping sharp teeth. It was all my fault! I watched and flapped and screeched all at once as she flicked the key in the lock and pulled the

door open. She wandered into the hall, and that was the end of Solstice. Or so I imagined, but after a fairly long while I  realised that she wasn't screaming as she was swallowed whole by the fang-beast, but instead was lazily wandering back into the room.

'There,' she said. 'Everything's quiet. Nothing to worry about. Just a bad dream.'

A bad dream? Is that all it had been? A nightmare. Had I still been asleep, and imagined the beast at the door?

'Everything's fine, Edgar. Now let's go to sleep, okay? It will all be all right in the morning, you'll see.'

But though Solstice might have been right about the dream, she was wrong about one thing.

It was not all right in the morning.

Thirteen

Flinch, Lord Valevine's most faithful retainer, has a secret desire to be an actor, a thing which is very unlikely to occur. His own mother stated that 'he has less appeal than you'd think possible.'

I never realised how many servants the castle had until that morning. Solstice and I had both slept late after the adventures of Wednesday, and as we came downstairs on Thursday, we were greeted by an extraordinary sight. The corridors, hallways and passages above ground level were heaving with people and things. There was a constant stream of carrying and lifting, and it was all very confusing, but as we reached the first floor gallery which overlooked the Small Hall, all became clear, because the hall was not there anymore.

What was there, was a lake. Quite a small lake, granted, but one that neatly filled the whole of the space which had until the evening before been the great entrance hall to Otherhand Castle.

Upon its surface floated all sorts of items; a top hat or two, flower arrangements, the odd servant, and other such fripperies. A rat swam by, looking confused.

Solstice stopped dead, and as she did, I instinctively departed her shoulder for a quick stretch of my wings. I was alarmed to see the water level approaching the top of the arch that led towards the dining hall, and judging the gap with a fine eye, I surged through it like a black arrow.

The situation in the dining hall was broadly similar, namely that it too was full of water. Peering down, I could see little, it was fairly murky, but I could just make out the top of the helmets on a couple of suits of armour that stood along the wall.

Mesmerised by the transformation of, it seemed, the entire ground floor of the castle, I tarried too long, for as I finally turned back towards the hall, I saw that my gap had closed. Gone. Entirely disappeared.

I circled near the archway, and thought briefly of kingfishers. I thought better of it. An underwater voyage could be fatal to the feather. I had only just got away with it yesterday, after all.

Frantically, I wheeled and saw in a blink of my beady eye that there were precious few perches left in the dining room. Time was running out, and, all windows shut, water continued to rise up the walls.

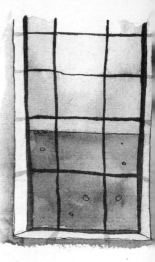

Ah ha! A plan formed. I could use the system of chimneys to exit the dining hall and find my way to somewhere less watery. But as I turned towards the massive fireplace, I saw that the top of the great mantelpiece was already underwater too.

I was about to give up all hope, when I saw something which rekindled it slightly. In the side of the hearth, high in the wall, was an air hole, designed to draw air into the chimney and vent smoke more successfully. It was small, but it was my only chance.

I darted towards it, scrambled in, took a few steps through an Edgar-sized tunnel of stone, and then was in space again. I flapped upwards as hard as I could, and felt the sooty walls of the chimney all about me. I had done it!

I was inside the chimney now. Beneath me I could smell water, but I could see nothing, for all was dark inside the flue. I pulled a few more wing beats, and suddenly hit my head on stone. I had reached the top of this branch of the chimney, where it turned a corner, before resuming its journey to the sky.

I scrambled sideways and found myself safe, resting in a horizontal branch of the vast network of chimneys that must run through the whole breadth and width, and height, of the castle.

I breathed heavily, coughing on the soot I had dislodged, and as I did so, I noticed two things.

First, I could see, ever so slightly. A pale grey light drifted down from some smoke stack way above me. Secondly, I could hear voices.

I stalked along my passageway, toward the source of the voices, which grew louder.

Then, the floor disappeared beneath me, and I dropped like a cannonball. I spotted daylight approaching beneath me, judged the moment, pulled on the air brakes, and shot out into the hallway again from the mouth of a fireplace on the first floor gallery.

I made quite a sight, I dare say, for even in the confusion of the gallery, I heard the sound of cabinets being dropped on toes, and the shriek of a pastry cook.

'Gasp!' I heard someone say, and knew that Solstice had witnessed my dramatic arrival, clouds of soot billowing around me, as I was still that cannonball, ushered in on a devilish waft of gun smoke.

'Oh! It's only Edgar.'

Only Edgar, I thought, a little hurt.

Only Edgar who has yet again defied death to bring news of the castle's doom.

Futhork.

No one paid me any more attention, and I landed on the balustrade of the gallery, and watched the discussion between Minty, Cook, Flinch and Solstice. Cudweed stood some way off, happily, I am sad to say, reunited with his idiotic primate.

'But who closed the door?'

'No one knows,' Cook said. 'But when I woke this morning to find my bed floating out of the servants' quarters, I thought maybe something was wrong.'

'I see,' said Minty. 'Very astute. And yet you failed to rescue any of my cake tins?'

'Mother!'

'We are working on the tins as we speak, your Ladyship,' said Flinch.

'Never mind cake tins,' Solstice exclaimed. 'What about the door? Never mind who shut it, what are we going to do about opening it again?'

No one answered this immediately, then Flinch bowed to Solstice.

'Begging your pardon, but we attempted to open the door when the water was still at waist height.'

Flinch's trousers were dripping wet, as was the tail of his flunkey coat.

'And?' said Solstice.

'It refused to move.'

'Refused?' cried Minty.

'It can't refuse. It's a door!'

'Nevertheless, Ma'am, we were unable to open it. Nor, I think I should add, were we able to open any other door, or window, on the ground floor of the castle. It seems the castle has decided, once again, not to cooperate. There is nowhere for the water to run away to, and hence, the castle is filling up.'

'Nonsense,' said Minty, but she said it in a small and unconvincing voice.

'It may be wise,' Flinch volunteered, 'to move things even higher into the castle. Perhaps the second, or third floors? Note, if you would be so kind, your feet.'

And then everyone began to panic and scream and talk all at once, for they had just noticed the water lapping around their toes.

Fourteen

Cudweed has many
other hobbies besides
monkeys; he's very
interested in food,
sleeping and being
scared. He also has a
stunning collection
of rodent skeletons.

The next hour or so was spent with more carrying and lifting and rushing and bustling.

Minty seemed to have vanished entirely. I suspect she went to His Lord and Ladyship's apartments on the fifth floor of the castle, and imagine she lay on the bed, clutching her forehead and bemoaning the rusting of her cake tins. In her absence, Cook took charge, directing Flinch, who in turn directed the removal of all precious items from the first floor, along with everything that had been rescued from the ground floor.

There was nothing to do but watch the show.

Cudweed and Solstice sat side by side on the wide

steps to the second floor, deep in discussion.
Cudweed had put Fellah on a lead, for which I
was very grateful. He explained that he couldn't
take the risk of the monkey escaping again, what
with rising water levels and toothsome monsters
on the prowl.

Let the chimp fend for
itself, that was my view, as it
sat pulling and tugging on
the string, obviously outraged
to be so close at paw without
being able to murder me.

I sat on the banister, at Solstice's side, in
case the monkey got loose. I knew she'd protect
me if she could.

'I don't understand,' Cudweed whimpered,

'why they couldn't just open the front door.'

'Nor does anyone else, brother dear, but there it is. The castle is refusing to budge. And the windows, too.'

'But why?'

Solstice shook her head.

'And,' persisted Cudweed, 'where is all the water coming from, anyway?'

A voice boomed from behind us.

'There are fearsome and fathomless places, my boy, of which you know nothing, and suspect even less!'

It was Valevine, descended from his tower of experimentation in a rare example of the thing known as Tea Break. He lifted a stiff finger and addressed the air more than

Cudweed, or even Solstice.

'And from deep within these occult
chambers all manner of things spring forth.
There are, for instance, subterranean water
courses, unseen and uncharted, deep under the
mountain upon which our castle rests. Flinch
and I have observed the egress of
these water courses, or rivers as
you might call them, from small
caves near the lakeside. And so it
is, that one of them must have
become diverted, and now seeks
to make its escape to the lake
via our home.

'That, my quaking boy, is
where the water is coming from.'

Cudweed tugged at the hem of his father's long coat.

'But, Father, why has the castle closed the doors? It's making the water stay in the castle.'

'That, my boy, I cannot say. But do not fear, because I am alert to the situation. Disastrous though it is, I shall temporarily interrupt my investigations into the thunder-producing-qualities-of-bull-frogs, and turn my flinty sharp mind to this latest problem at hand. All will be well!'

'So what shall we do?' Solstice asked.

'Eh? What's that, my girl, my first born child?'

'I said, so what shall we do? Actually?'

Valevine rose an inch or two on his tip toes, as if about to make a shattering announcement, then sank again on his heels.

'Well,' he said, quietly, 'what would be, er, would what . . . I mean, what do you think?'

'Open the windows higher up the castle?'

'Precisely!' snapped Valevine. 'Exactly so! Well, come on then. Let's get on to it!'

Cudweed and Solstice scrambled to their feet and dodging round maids and footmen loaded down with paintings, rugs and books, they skipped away to open some first floor windows.

I set off after them, but by the time I was entering the first room, Solstice was already on her way out. I saw Cudweed in another room, struggling with a window, and then bumped into Solstice again.

'It's no good!' she cried.

She ran off down the hall, and I heard her shouting for help, trying every window as she went.

'It's no good. They won't open!'

More lamenting, bemoaning and general chattering broke out then, everyone tried, and failed, to open a single window on the first floor.

'Wait!' called Solstice. 'Supposing we broke one?'

'What?' cried Cudweed, 'I'd get in such trouble!'

'No!' Solstice said. 'I'll say I told you to do it. I'll take the blame. Just smash that window!'

She pointed at an ornate stained glass window overlooking the valley.

'Excellent!' declared Cudweed. Being told to break a window on purpose was probably very near the top of his all time wish list, and so with great excitement, Cudweed snatched a mace from the mailed fist of a suit of armour, and swung it at the window.

I flinched, everyone ducked, waiting for the crash, but it never came. The mace bounced harmlessly off the glass.

There was a small silence, a moment of pause.

'Try another one!' Solstice said, urging Cudweed on.

He tried another one, with the same result.

Suddenly everyone was throwing everything they could get their hands on at the glass. I took this as a sign to be out of human reach, and winged my way up to the ceiling.

Suddenly, having failed to even scratch a single pane of glass, everyone fled the room, crying and calling to each other.

'The castle's trying to kill us!'

'We're doomed to drown!'

'Doomed!'

That kind of thing.

Anyway, I followed Solstice and Cudweed as they scurried back down the corridor to their father, who still stood imperiously on the steps up from the gallery.

'Well?' he enquired, melodiously.

'We can't do it, Father!' Solstice panted. 'All the windows are shut tight.'

'We even tried to smash them!' shouted Cudweed, grinning in a moment of dare-devilishness.

Valevine shot Cudweed a glance from under one arched eyebrow, and he started cowering again, in appropriate fashion.

'I see,' drawled Lord Otherhand, very, very slowly. 'I. See.' He jutted his chin, and as it is a decent sized chin, it looked fairly impressive. He dragged his gaze around the shrinking walls of his ancestral home, and nodded his head slightly.

'So,' he whispered. 'It is like this, is it?'

Around us, everything was ruckus and noise, as word of the sealed nature of the castle spread from maid to footman and butler to kitchen boy. My beak twitched of its own accord. I tried to settle it but could not. A sure sign of nerves, and still I knew that my hour was at hand. My duty called, and I would answer that call.

So I prepared for action, but then, there

came an ear splitting scream, a wail as of the banshee of legend perhaps. A scream which penetrated and nearly burst every ear drum in the castle.

Two dozen pairs of eyes turned to see the source of the sound, and there was Minty, Lady Otherhand, standing at the top of the flight of steps, staring at something down in the water in the hall. Her eyes were round, her lips still trembling from the scream. Her arm lifted, slowly, slowly, slowly, and she uncurled and extended her forefinger, as if in a nightmare, to point at something she had seen.

Two dozen pairs of eyes swung back to the surface of the indoor lake.

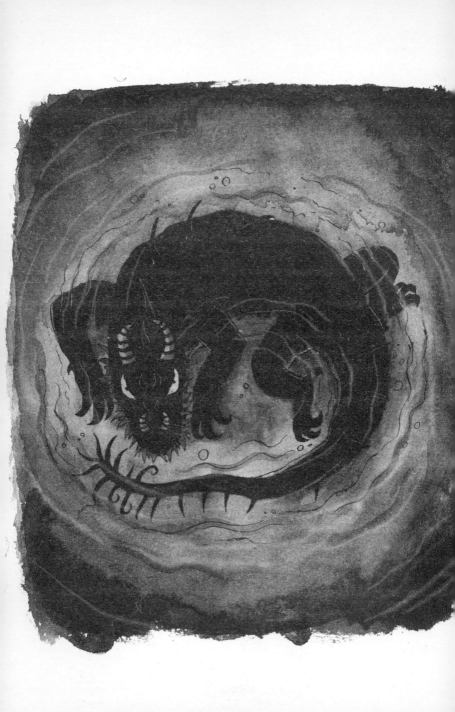

There, drifting through the water, as merry as you please, was the thing. The **fang-beast**. It was the length of a horse, with the head of a snake, but with ten times the teeth, and a fat scaly body. It swished along on four chubby legs and with the flick of its tail, which now that I saw it for a second awful time, looked like nothing but the tail of a dragon.

It circled a couple of times, as if deciding where to go next, and seemed unaware of twenty-three mouths and one beak gawping at it from the relative security of the gallery.

Then, all of a sudden, the beast opened its mouth and gave the most almighty belch that has ever been heard in God's Kingdom.

A second later, something shot out of the

beast's mouth and landed twenty feet ahead of it, making a small splash that broke the silence.

It was a pair of boots.

They stayed on the surface for no more than a breath, and then sank slowly out of sight.

'Has anyone seen Alice?' someone said, and then twenty-two pairs of feet, two pairs of monkey-feet-hands, and one pair of wings, all fled for the stairs and the higher reaches of the castle, and with it, safety.

But safety for how long?

Fifteen

It's said that the Deffreeques practised the dark arts, such as necromancy, thaumaturgy and osteopathy. The Otherhands don't; they're good enough without the practice.

It was a long and wearisome afternoon. After the stampede to the second floor had ended, and someone pointed out that the beast had not come shimmying up the stairs after us, and someone else wondered aloud whether it was digesting Alice, and a third someone told the second someone to shut up, boredom kicked in.

After a couple of hours of sitting around, waiting to be eaten, it's remarkable how quickly monotony overtakes mortal fear. So, by the time lunch should have happened, and hadn't, there was universal agreement that we may as well go on moving things higher into the castle, and so every pair of hands in the castle set to moving things up another floor.

Well, almost every pair of hands. The three notable absences were Lord Valevine, her Ladyship, and Fellah. But no one likes a monkey touching their stuff anyway.

It was around this time that someone remembered Grandmother Slivinkov, Minty's mother, and a bunch of quaking footmen was sent with a sedan chair to fetch her from her lair. They made quite a sight as they returned, and set off upstairs into the highest reaches of the castle, to find an attic even higher than the one she spends all her time in.

Four flunkeys each at a corner of the sedan chair, and perched upon it was old lady Silvinkov herself, a tiny shrivelled creature with long grey hair but with eyes that could still have you for breakfast at a hundred paces.

They passed by and I quivered.

Then boredom returned.

As I watched the work progress, I wondered idly why it seemed to me that there was more of this sort of thing going on than ever before. By 'this sort of thing', I don't mean furniture lifting, I mean Oddness. Strange visitors, ghostly sightings, mysterious noises. Maybe I'm imagining things, but it's my belief that something is definitely up at the moment. Something I cannot quite stick my beak in.

I'm an old hand at these things; by which I mean
Trouble at Castle Otherhand, but I have to admit,
I'm stumped. There is an undercurrent of badness
that I cannot fully fathom.

I digress.

I watched the procession of cupboards
and chairs wind on up the staircase. I
could do little to help, not being
blessed with hands, but I hopped
about in an encouraging fashion,
and gave the odd cheery squawk to
Cudweed and Solstice as they carried
eye-high piles of books upstairs.

Maybe it was because they hadn't had any
lunch, or maybe because they were tired, and
maybe a little scared, but in a show of rare

affection for the boy, I hopped onto Cudweed's head.

'**Kawk!**' I told him, which in the dignified tongue of the raven is a useful word that can mean many things, and which in this case, meant 'there, there, poor young thing, I'm sorry to see you so troubled.'

Maybe it was from tiredness and hunger and fear, but Cudweed took an almighty swing at me with a chubby fist. I flapped aside, but he still caught one wing, and I hobbled to Solstice for support.

'**Arruk!**' I told her, which can loosely be translated as 'Hey!' and hopped onto her head instead.

'**Kawk!**' I told her, and then to my

great unhappiness, she did the same as her petulant younger brother, and angrily brushed me off.

'Edgar!' she cried. 'Can't you leave us alone for one minute! We're trying to save the castle and you're just getting in the way!'

Well, my feathers nearly fell out there and then.

I didn't need telling again. Forlornly, I fluttered to the floor and began to stalk off down the corridor, striking, I felt, a posture of noble pain.

'Ha ha! Look!'

Cudweed's irritating cackle came from over my shoulder.

'Look at old Pointy Beak! He's walking!

How silly he looks!'

Well, that was enough. It had been foolish of me to walk in front of the human species, and I took wing again, speeding from the second floor corridor to the stairs in an instant.

As I went, I vaguely heard Solstice speaking to Cudweed.

'Oh,' she said, 'You don't think we upset him, do you?'

'Don't be silly. He's only an old bird, isn't he?'

'Yes,' said Solstice, 'I suppose you're right.'

I was thoroughly fed up, Guardian of Otherhand or not. I would definitely run away, leave the lot of them to drown, and find a new castle to belong to, with a nicer set of people living in it.

People who would say nicer things to me, like how clever I was, or how black my feathers were, or how strong my beak was. Ravens like to hear that kind of thing every now and then.

With that goal in mind, I decided to explore the whole of the castle that was not yet submerged, with a view to finding a way out. All I needed was one, small, raven-sized hole, and I would be free.

Somewhere, there had to be a tiny chink in the castle's skin. A single broken pane of glass, a terrace door that stood ajar, an air vent, or . . . yes! Of course! I'd already been close to my escape route that very day.

The chimneys!

But, oh! The thought of those tiny dark soot-lined tubes! Ugh!

Could I do it, could I really do it?

Yes, I could. All I had to do was fly to the top of the castle, to a room with a chimney near the roof, and my journey would be a relatively short one. A snappy burst of wing power, and I'd be free. There and then a picture came into my head of my daring escape, as I shot like a black rocket into the clear blue air of the valley.

So be it!

I got as far as the fifth floor, trying to find an open door, when I found what I was after, and dropping to the floor, crept into the room. It was only when I was inside that I realised where I was. It was the private rooms of Lord and

Lady Otherhand. There's only one suite more off-limits than theirs, and that is the murky boudoir of Grandmother Slivinkov.

Never mind, I told myself, one chimney is as good as another. I stole through the antechamber, saw another open door, which from dim memory I knew led to the bedroom, and a bedroom that would certainly have a fireplace, and behind that fireplace, an escape route.

I was halfway across the Turkish rug, when a syrupy voice caught me.

'Edgar! Dear bird.'

I turned. It was her Ladyship.

'We don't see much of you up here, these days, do we Edgar?'

No, we do not, I thought, since you and your husband are in your different ways both dangerously potty.

In one hand she held a handkerchief, and in the other, some piece of cooking equipment, I wasn't sure what.

'Look!' she cried, so suddenly, that I nearly jumped out of my feathery coat. 'Look! This is all I have left of my prize collection of cake tins. This laughable muffin tray! Oh, what is to become of my hopes now?'

She sat down on the bed emitting various noises of great distress, and shoved the handkerchief into her face.

'Come here, dear bird. Come and sit with me.'

I looked around the room nervously, but there was no option.

I jumped onto the bed next to her, and suffered her to stroke my neck feathers. I tilted my head and looked sideways at her. She seemed very old to me, even though I was many times her age, but I suppose I suddenly thought that she looked old, in human terms. Stupid old woman, I thought. Her home is being destroyed, her servants are being eaten one by one, there's every chance her children will be next, and all she can think about is her cake tins.

'I suppose you think,' she said, 'that all I think about is cakes? Not so, Edgar, there are other things, too. Important things. Biscuits and breads, for particular example, and baking in general.'

That was it. I looked about for the chimneybreast, when she spoke again.

'And even more important than baking, there's people. People you love. People you don't want to see in trouble.'

I stopped in my tracks, unable to believe my ears. The old bat had surely finally lost her lentils! But no, for she continued her little speech.

'And it makes me quite, quite sad, Edgar dear, to think of Solstice and my little Cudweed getting eaten by that thing, and drowned if not eaten. And then there's his Lordship. I suppose I must have loved him once upon a time. I think it would be quite sad if he were to be chewed by that . . . (she gasped) . . . thing I saw in the water. Wouldn't it?'

Yes, I thought, it would be.

'**Urk!**' I said, '**Urk! Kawk!**'

'Hmm,' she went on, dreamily, 'what's that, dear? Anyway, I just don't know what to do. The water is rising, the beast is prowling, and I don't suppose anyone had the slightest thought of saving any food from the kitchens before they went underwater. My poor little Cudweed can't go without lunch *and* dinner. He'll starve before breakfast.'

Feed him to the monster and we'll all have two nights reprieve, I thought. Or rather, that was my first thought, and then, it was swept aside by another thought, and I cursed myself for being such a foolish, sentimental old bird.

'Yes,' she continued, 'People. They're more important than cake tins. Well, maybe almost as important.'

And with that, I burst from Minty's clutches, and sped for the chimney. Three wing beats later, I tasted sweet fresh air, and I soared up into the blue, blue sky.

Sixteen

Once every twelve years, Edgar disappears from the castle for two weeks. Only he knows where he goes, but it's become such a habit it's known to everyone in the castle as Edgar's holiday.

Drat the lot of them! Drat!

Rude, uncaring, impolite, selfish, deranged, obstinate, mean, tiresome, smelly and so very, very unfeathered. Hah!

I circled up and up into the early evening air, going higher and higher, so that the castle got smaller and smaller beneath me. It had been a beautifully clear, sunny day, and there was no more than a wisp of cloud for me to cut through as I made my way to dizzying heights, as dusk fell. I flew on, up and up, until the air began to thin, so that it was hard for my wings to find a grip on it, and hard for my little old lungs to suck in enough of the stuff.

In a state of exhaustion, I glided, rising again where I found a late updraft of warm air from the valley so far below.

I gazed down at the lake, and its shining surface, and I reflected.

My lot was a strange one.

I had lived in the valley for so many years. I had been there before the Otherhand family stole the castle from the Deffreeques, and I had been there when fifteen generations before the Deffreeques had built the thing in the first place, and even then I was not a young bird.

Ask an ornithologist what the lifespan of a raven is, and they will tell you with smug certainty that the raven lives for twenty years in the wild, maybe twice as long in captivity. So tell me then how it is that I can remember seeing the ancient oak on the far side of the valley when it sprouted from an acorn. I have seen countless people come and go. Once upon a time, I had poor Mrs Edgar for company, but even those days are long behind me now. Am I a freak? Are there other birds like me, who have lived for such an incredibly long time? Am I some magical being? Am I indeed immortal?

No, I don't think I am, for I am getting old at last. I hurt when I fly for too long. My neck gets terribly stiff these days, and I feel the rheumatism in my joints. If that monkey got me, I would stop being immortal in about three seconds, and it is not something I am going to experiment with.

I don't know the answer, but as I circled high above the castle, I was in two minds.

One part of me looked down and saw the people, and even the castle itself, as insignificant. People came and went, they lived their little lives, and then died, whether by being eaten, or starving, or drowning. In the end it didn't matter much. And looked at like that, it was hard to feel much sorrow for the plight of the Otherhands and their many and ludicrous retainers.

But another part of me saw things differently. A part of me that felt sorry for them. For their foolishness, and stupidity. I realised that this part of me cared about them, about Solstice, even though she'd been mean to me, a part of me saw that even mad old Minty had a heart somewhere inside her flowery bosom, a part of me that feared even for Cudweed, and I knew then that I would never forgive myself if anything bad were to happen.

I took one last circle, tipped my tail feathers up and my beak down, and hurtled back to earth with a determination to save them all, Valevine, Minty, Solstice, Cook, Flinch, every last parlour maid and boot boy, and even Cudweed.

The monkey, however, could go to hell.

Seventeen

Nanny Lumber is a
fearsome, foul and
flatulent figure, the
terror of the castle,
even Lord Valevine
often about-turns
when he sees her
thundering down
the corridor.

S olstice had been right.

It was a mystery, and it
needed solving. And now,
I was the only one with the power
to solve it, for the simple reason that I was the
only one who could leave the castle.

In a wild spin, I tried to remember
things about mysteries, and how they get solved,
and within a single ruffle of feathers came to
the conclusion that I knew nothing about
them whatsoever.

I was still plummeting, and
strange though this may sound, I find
that plummeting is good thinking time,
even though it is, by the nature of the
direction of a plummet, limited in its duration.

I was maybe halfway back to the castle, when I realised that I had several pieces of information in my possession already.

They seemed like pieces of a jigsaw puzzle, and with sudden delight I remembered that a police detective would have called them by a magical word: clues.

I had some clues, three in all.

First, there was the monster, as evidenced by various missing kitchen maids.

Second, there was the water.

And third, there was the rockfall in the cave mouth.

All three had arrived at around the same time, and with one of those flashes of inspiration you can only have when plummeting, I saw that all these events were connected.

'Futhork!' I screeched, not only at my genius, but also because I had run out of plummeting room, and was about to be dashed upon the flags of the courtyard. I stuck my wings out as hard as I could, and pulled myself into a horizontal glide, though the force as I did so was nearly enough to have my wings off.

I looked for somewhere to rest and spied the pointy bit on the rotunda roof. Perfect thinking spot!

I saw it all. The whole thing, a series of events, that connected back into the past, and would connect forwards to the future unless I, the hero of the piece, did something about it very soon.

So! The creature had arrived, by way of the immeasurable and ancient caves and tunnels on which the castle was built, lured to the surface by the scent of small boys and grease-stained kitchen maids, and had begun

to snack upon this bountiful supply of food. To
be honest, this might have been happening for
quite some time before anyone noticed. There
are so many maids that it's a miracle anyone
spotted Ishbel had gone astray. Then there was
the water, and the rockfall. But supposing these
things had happened the other way around?
Suppose there had been other rockfalls, deep
under the castle that had blocked the path of

the underground rivers that Valevine had spoken of? With the exit blocked, the water had begun to back up inside the caves, then blocked again by the rockfall I had myself seen, and now, with the water rising into the cellar, there was only one way left for it, and the fang beast, to go. Into the castle!

And now, here was my final piece of understanding. It was the castle itself that was doing it. And as evidence for that, I need only point to the fact that the castle had itself shut all its windows, and all its doors, so that the water could not escape.

The castle was trying to rid itself of the creature, trying to drown it, flush it out. Stupid castle! Maybe, it was trying to help, but in doing so, it was going to drown every one of its occupants.

I looked down between my talons and saw that the whole of the rotunda beneath me was filled with water. How long had I been gone? If the rotunda was filled, that meant the third floor at least had to have gone under.

I flapped off the pointy bit and despairing, circled the entire castle. What I saw terrified me. Otherhand seemed full of water, pressing against every window, like a vast fish tank, as I flew higher it seemed every floor had gone. The castle was some awful version of Noah and his Ark, only this time the water was on the inside, with the animals.

The castle was by no means a perfectly water-tight drum, and little jets of water squeaked out between window frames here, and cracks in the masonry there, but as fast as these holes let the water out, the underground river pumped more in.

Solstice! I thought wildly. Have you perished?

I soared to the highest point in the whole castle, and there I took my usual perch, on the window ledge outside 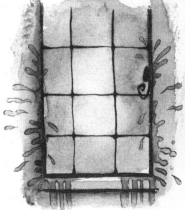 Valevine's laboratory in the East Tower.

I peered through the glass and nearly stepped back off the window ledge in surprise.

Inside the round room, was every single inhabitant of Castle Otherhand, squashed in so there was barely room to breathe, let alone stand.

Despite the small size of the room, everyone seemed to be pushing themselves back and away from the door, from which there came a persistent scraping and thumping.

There was screaming in the room, a lot of screaming in fact, and a bit of shouting too.

This was it!

The end of the Otherhand dynasty approached, with flood and fang.

Eighteen

Along with kitchen maids, the castle also gets through more than its fair share of schoolmasters, creating frequent interruptions to the children's education, filled in haphazard fashion by their father's lectures . . .

Like a bird possessed, I banged on the window with my beak. That can make a pretty sharp noise, I assure you, and yet with all the noise in the laboratory, I had trouble making anyone hear me.

The scrabbling at the door, the only door into the room, grew louder, and I had visions of the beast going crazy with hunger and a lust for blood. Inside the room, I could make out Valevine and Flinch, Minty and Cook, Solstice (hooray!), Cudweed and Fellah (oh well, another time, maybe), all squashed in among the entire serving staff of the castle, or those left uneaten, at least.

Grandmother Slivinkov still sat motionless and stony-faced atop her sedan chair, still carried by four exhausted footmen. Valevine was shouting at two bootboys and a scullery maid who were sending his equipment crashing to the floor, as they clambered onto tables and workbenches, in the feeble hope that that would save them when the time came.

That time seemed to be coming soon, I could see the wood of the rickety old door starting to splinter. At each crash, the wailing and shrieking rose another few decibels more desperate.

Adding to the chaos, were Valevine's bullfrogs, which, their cages trampled underfoot, were hopping and croaking and putting the wind up kitchen and parlour maid alike, with no sign that their croaking was going to cause any kind of meteorological activity whatsoever, let alone a clap of thunder or lightning bolt.

Another bang on the door, and then I distinctly heard Solstice.

'Gasp!' she said, 'There's water coming under the door!'

Well, that was it. The whole room went berserk for a good five minutes, during which time I hopped and flapped about like a cat in treacle. Still no one heard me, until, someone, or rather something, finally did.

Fellah.

He screeched like an attention-seeking seagull and the whole room looked round to see what he'd seen. Me.

'Oh!' Solstice cried, 'Edgar!'

'Never mind him!' Valevine replied. 'We have bigger fish to fry!'

I didn't much care for being compared to fish, but I suppose the gist of what he said was true.

Nevertheless, Solstice pushed her way through the crowd to the window, trying once more to open it, but without luck. I noticed now that the water was ankle-high, because a rather miserable frog floated between Solstice's legs as she stood by the window and talked to me.

'Edgar,' she said. 'You came back!'

She seemed really pleased to see me.

'Edgar, there's something I have to say to you. I'm sorry. I was mean to you, and I shouldn't have been. I know you were only trying to help, really, but I was mean. I'm really sorry.'

She pushed her face right up against the glass, so close to my beak, yet so far.

'I wanted you to know that, before . . . Well, you know, before the door gets broken down.'

I might have wept, but there was no time, because the banging on the door grew ever louder. Presumably, outside in the narrow passage, the beast was up to its gizzards in water, and though it might swim for a while, would also shortly drown when the water reached the ceiling of this, the highest spot in the whole castle.

Driven by the frantic combination of food ahead of it and water behind it, the beast renewed its attack on the woodwork of the laboratory door, and then, with an almighty splintering crack, its head shoved through a fairly neat little hole about a foot from the floor.

I shall leave you to
wonder for yourself at the
almost unimaginable din of
a couple of dozen people,
and one small but very
loud monkey, upon
seeing the jaws of
a snapping
monster protrude
through a hole
in a door no
more than a few
feet away.

The monster was an **abomination**.

Up close it was more terrifying than I
could ever have believed. When Solstice said she

suspected it had more than the one fang we
found, she'd really hit the nail on the head.
The creature from the caves had at least three
rows of mean,
curving teeth,
the one set
inside the
other, so that
there seemed
no room for
anything else in that mouth, other than teeth.
And yet that, I thought rather gloomily, was
where poor Ishbel, Ann, and Alice, had disappeared,
down that snapping and slurping gullet. Ooh!
The beast's eyes were set far back and
wide apart on its broad slimy head, so that it

seemed it could look in opposite directions at once, which I supposed, also a little morbidly I know, was very handy when catching a running boot boy.

Ooh, again!

And then, then I noticed something, something which was slowly dawning on the yelping occupants of the laboratory; although the monster had succeeded in shoving its head through a hole in the door, it had not succeeded in forcing the door to give way any further. Nor had it bounded into the room like a cross between a beast from hell and a deranged Labrador puppy, ready to devour anything that was warm and moving.

The thing was, in fact, stuck.

Wriggling aplenty, snapping, most terribly, and yet, stuck.

'Look!' said Solstice, ever the sharpest of the Otherhand clan. 'It's stuck.'

'It may be, my dear daughter,' said Valevine, 'but note this. We are also stuck, and the water continues to trouble us.'

What his Lordship said was true, for the water had by now reached knee height, and I could see nothing but an untidy end to the situation.

But as, from my safer vantage point, I viewed their predicament, yet another mighty plan entered the corridors of my raven brain.

It was a thought that didn't have words,

not at first, it was more in the way of a picture, as I remembered something I had seen in this very room, very recently. I recalled some of the unpleasantness that Valevine had been inflicting upon the amphibians of Otherhand, and then that picture shifted slightly, and I saw that same dreadful apparatus being lifted and placed over the head of the upsetting organism at the door.

Now, I must say, I'm not proud of what I saw in my little black head, but it wasn't the time to wonder too much at the darker side of my nature. I knew I had to put the plan into action.

But how? As I think I have mentioned before, ravens are not blessed with hands. I had to get someone else to see the same thing that I had.

Like a shot, I was off that window ledge, so fast that I swear Solstice thought I had dematerialised. In two short sweeps of flight, I was surging down the small chimney into the laboratory, thanking the stars that whoever had built this Tower had felt the need for a fireplace, small though it was.

I arrived like a bullet, and darted straight to the workbench, where the largest of Valevine's experimental bell jars sat, teetering on the edge. I began to peck at it for all I was worth, and to help me do this I simply imagined that the jar was Fellah's cranium. The monkey, I noticed, was cowering and clinging to Cudweed's neck, so I was safe enough, though in truth, I did not at the moment fear for my own safety.

I had more important work to do.

So I pecked at the jar, with every confidence that they would grasp my plan, and swing into action.

'Look,' said Cudweed. 'Edgar's gone mental.'

'**Futhork!**' I cried. Just how stupid *were* these people?

I took a deep breath, and flapped from the bell jar, over to the snapping jaws of Death itself, narrowly avoiding an upward lunge by the beast's head, and losing two tail feathers in the process. Now I danced with danger, hopping about between the

monster's eyes, behind those rows of chomping teeth. Then, back to the jar, and back to the beast, and now, now finally, Solstice spoke.

'I think,' she said, 'he wants us to put the jar over its head. But what's the point of that?'

'Yes,' said Valevine, excitedly. 'No. Yes, I mean yes . . . Ah-ha! I have it! I have a wonderful idea!

We connect the pump!'

Exhausted, I flapped up to perch on a beam in the roof, and watched as Valevine took control of the situation, as if it had all been his idea.

I gazed almost dreamily as they manoeuvred

the bell jar into place over those snapping, slavering

jaws. It fitted like a glove, no room to spare.

Well, I told myself, it was what I had wanted.

I had wanted them to understand me for once,

and they actually had,

somehow,

between

them,

figured

it

out.

I watched as they attached the massive hoses to the valves on the side of the bell jar, and then, at a wave from Valevine, Flinch and one of the under butlers began gravely to pump the handle.

Within a fraction of a second, the rubber base of the bell jar sucked itself to the door, sealing the beast's doom.

Slowly and steadily, Flinch and the under butler bent to their task, and as they did so the pressure inside the jar rose and rose. Just about then I thought it might be an idea to look away. I shuffled up to the far end of my beam, took one last look over my shoulder at the hideous deformation occurring inside the bell jar, and tucked my beak under my wing.

The last thing I saw was a roomful of people, all craning forward in rapt anticipation, horrified but fascinated by the strange changes happening under the glass. I suppose I could have warned them, but they probably wouldn't have understood anyway. They never do.

I heard Valevine.

'Now, Flinch! The valve!'

Then there was that disgusting sucking plop that I had heard before, from the frogs, only ten times worse. At the same moment, it seemed the glass was unable to withstand the sudden release of pressure from inside, and it exploded.

There was the sound of something spraying all over the room, and untucking my beak, I noticed that everyone was quietly covered in red goo.

I seemed to be free of the stuff, high up on my little perch, but then I noticed a drop of it on my right talon.

I bent down and licked it off.

'Oh, Edgar, that's disgusting,' cried Solstice.

No, I thought, actually it's not too bad.

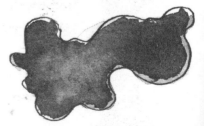

Nineteen

The presence of
ghosts in Castle
Otherhand has never
been proven for sure,
but everyone agrees
the noises from the
South Wing are
heard more and
more often.

It was like a miracle. Perhaps it even was. And what happened next was proof that I had indeed put the pieces of that jigsaw puzzle together in the right order.

Almost as soon as the monster had evaporated, the castle decided that all was well again, and allowed its doors to spring open. Windows suddenly popped wide, and the water level began to drop rapidly.

'Not so fast!' cried Valevine, and he did the strangest thing. He jumped over to

the door and yanked it open, dodging
the remains of the back end of the beast,
and flung himself into the sinking
flood waters.

Now we saw what he was up to,
for he, like everyone else in the room
but me, was covered in goo.

'The largest bath in the world!'
he cried. 'Don't miss it! Someone's pulled the
plug out!'

By now the water had retreated to the
fourth floor landing, and everyone dived in,
swimming and treading water and having a bath
and washing their clothes all at the same time.

All except Fellah, who, though
covered in slime, refused to wash.

Refused until, that is, Cudweed grabbed him by the neck and dragged him into the water.

'Come on, Fellah,' he said, 'Nobody likes a sticky monkey.' Truer words were never spoken.

So, the water went, and though it left behind a damp and somewhat muddy castle, it washed away everyone's fear of the beast, too.

People were laughing and calling to each other, as they showed off, doing backstroke across the dining room, until finally the water left the castle, even the cellars, for good.

Everyone stood around, congratulating Valevine on his equipment, and on his quick thinking.

'Ah yes,' he acknowledged. 'The work of

the scientist is lonely at times, but we suffer for the benefit of others. And yet, I must not take all the credit.'

If I had actual ears, they would at this point have pricked up.

'For indeed, I was helped today, and there is someone else we should thank.'

'Yes, yes!' everyone cried.

'Yes,' said Valevine. 'Flinch! Step forward my man!'

I flew away to sulk, but as I did so, I saw Solstice standing in the doorway. She smiled at me and put out her arm, and rather ungraciously, I landed on it, tramping heavily to show her I was not in the best of moods.

She laughed. She smiled at me, and I felt my darkness lighten a little.

'Don't worry, Edgar,' she whispered. 'I won't ever forget who really saved us.'

And with that, she kissed the very tip of my beak, and, deep inside, I grinned a secret raven grin.

Postscript

It may have occurred to you, as it occurred to no one else during the Great Flood of Otherhand, to wonder what happened to Nanny Lumber during those wettest of times. For she was left in her sick bed all the while, and only when the waters subsided did anyone think to see if she was all right. I am unhappy to report that she was absolutely fine, and rather grumpily said she hadn't noticed that her bedroom was full of water, a statement which has made everyone question what species she belongs to just that little bit more.

Following Flood and Fang, Edgar reveals all in

Ghosts and Gadgets
Lunatics and Luck
Magic and Mayhem
Vampires and Volts
Diamonds and Doom